SHADOW OF THE PROTECTOR

Recent Titles by Elizabeth Lord

THE BOWMAKER GIRLS
FOR ALL THE BRIGHT PROMISE
MILE END GIRL
THE TURNING TIDES

BUTTERFLY SUMMERS *
AUTUMN SKIES *
WINTER WINE *

* *available from Severn House*

SHADOW OF THE PROTECTOR

Elizabeth Lord

This first world edition published in Great Britain 2002 by
SEVERN HOUSE PUBLISHERS LTD of
9–15 High Street, Sutton, Surrey SM1 1DF.
This first world edition published in the USA 2002 by
SEVERN HOUSE PUBLISHERS INC of
595 Madison Avenue, New York, N.Y. 10022.

British Library Cataloguing in Publication Data

Lord, Elizabeth
Shadow of the Protector
1. Cromwell, Oliver – Family
2. Great Britain – History – Commonwealth and Protectorate, 1649–1660 – Fiction
3. Love stories
I. Title
823.9′14 [F]

ISBN 0-7278-5825-4

Typeset by Palimpsest Book Production Ltd.,
Polmont, Stirlingshire, Scotland.
Printed and bound in Great Britain by
MPG Books Ltd., Bodmin, Cornwall.

One

1649

It was cold, a brittle cold day. During the night there had been a brief flurry of snow, the flakes now fixed by a fierce and persistent frost. The last but one day of January and a bitter one it had been too – in ways other than weather.

Frances Cromwell twisted sideways a little on the small window seat and with the tip of one forefinger coaxed a clear round patch in the frost coating on one diamond pane of the tiny casement window, the tip of her finger chilling in unison with the widening patch.

Peeping wistfully through the clear hole she'd made, she could see the palely gleaming pavement. The crooked rooftops of King Street were still half cloaked in shadow even at midday, the sun so low, its slanting rays struggling through the smoke haze from London's innumerable hearths.

The cobbled road was brown with horse droppings. Hooves and the wheels of carts and carriages had melted frost and light snow to a thin slush but in odd corners and on windowsills the soft round flakes had piled up into tiny pure white mounds, untouched, glistening beckoningly.

She allowed herself a long, yearning sigh. Oh, to put on a cape and hood, venture out to play, gather up one small handful of the meagre, virgin snow and form a minuscule snowball to throw it as far as she could. But today no children played in the street. All pleasures had been forbidden and the faces of the few passers-by had set expressions as, huddled against the biting cold, they hurried in the direction of nearby Whitehall.

Frances glanced at her sister sitting beside her. Mary had her head lowered. Her dark brown ringlets, fallen forward over the soft round face, concealed the arched eyebrows, the dark teasing eyes and the soft rounded jawline. Hands clasped in her lap, one thumbnail was toying idly with the other. Beneath the hands a small bible lay open at the Book of Job but was for the moment forgotten.

Cautiously, Frances bent towards her. 'I can't see why we mayn't occupy ourselves with something other than reading,' she whispered, a wary eye trained upon their mother seated in the high-backed chair that their father usually used.

The big family bible lay open before her on the dark oak table. A page rustled in the quiet room as it was turned. Seated on smaller back-stools nearer the warmth of the hearth were Frances' older sisters, Bridget and Betty. Twenty years old and sweet-natured, Betty shared nothing in common with her dour sister five years her senior but seeming even older with her tight, prim little mouth and her cold grey humourless eyes.

On this day both were without their husbands. At this very moment Bridget's husband, Henry Ireton, and Betty's, John Claypole, were at Whitehall at the side of their father-in-law, Cromwell, as was their place today, their wives left here at home to pray for the King's soul.

Bridget, stiff-faced as ever, was doing her praying to the utmost, hands tightly clasped before her bosom, head bowed – a statue fixed in permanent devotion.

Betty, on the other hand, was dividing her time alternately reading her own small bible and sighing, her brows occasionally knitting against a persistent pain which she said was caused by her irregular periodic flow. Not that she allowed it to ever spoil her natural good humour, but today her pleasing countenance was marred by the solemnity of this occasion.

None of the women appeared disturbed by the whispered comment from Frances, and guardedly watching her mother's sallow, flat features, she was prompted to greater boldness, still keeping her voice down.

'Were we to be allowed to do our embroidery the time might go a little quicker.'

Mary, almost thirteen years old, a little over eighteen months older than she and therefore seeing herself as wiser, gave Frances a sideways glance of disapproval from under lowered brows. Her expression lugubrious as befitted this sombre occasion, her full youth-red lips were for once drawn thin. 'It wouldn't be proper on such a day, Frankie,' she whispered back.

'Oh, la-la!' Frances derided, but she was careful to keep her jeer low for fear of censure by her mother or Bridget. When none came she reverted to her earlier complaint. 'I swear, Mall, the hours drag twice as slow, sitting here in idleness.'

'I don't think they are dragging for *him*,' Mary replied ominously, causing Frances to regard her with dread speculation, her own pretty face lengthening. Her somewhat heavy-lidded eyes, so like Mary's, widened with her vision of what was soon to happen.

'Oh, Mall, how awful it must be to—'

A half burned log in the hearth collapsing into the fire, sending a shower of sparks up the chimney, made Frances jump at the sudden interruption to the quietness of the parlour.

Settling back to her own imagination, still careful to keep her voice down, Frances went on, 'He must be terribly afraid. I would be too if I were about to be executed in less than an hour from now.' Her words flowed faster and with less caution in keeping with her vision of it all. 'To have to walk out from Whitehall Palace and into that cold and kneel with all the crowd looking on and have to lay my neck on that block . . .'

'Frances!' Her mother's tone, low yet sharp, made her jump more violently than had the collapsing of the log in the grate. 'If you must dwell on the King's fate, then pray for his soul rather than revel in his plight.'

Obediently, Frances bent her head but no prayer came. Only thought of her father, the Lieutenant General Cromwell. He was most likely with King Charles at this very moment. What were her father's own thoughts on this dreadful business at this very moment? Was he speaking to that self-willed man, beseeching him even in this final hour to bow to the authority of Parliament, or had he withdrawn to his rooms in Whitehall to brood upon the dread import of that decision he had finally been compelled to make? So many questions ran through her head as she visualised her father, stern and tight-lipped, perhaps standing at a window overlooking the scaffold.

She'd glimpsed the half completed structure from a coach when she had gone to Cheapside with her mother to purchase some black braid a few days earlier. Between the close-set buildings had come the sight of the wide square and in front of the great Banqueting Hall the bones of the scaffold supporting the block where the King would die under the headman's axe.

Tales had reached her ears – street rumours of course, regaled by Polly their housemaid to Mrs Pearson their cook, heard from some delivery boy who in turn had heard it all from heaven knows where – how the disciplinarian Cromwell had watched every last timber hammered into place; how he'd delighted in signing the King's death warrant; how he was said to have pressed the pen-hand of one dithering Parliamentarian to the document until the man's signature had been added to those already on the document, and how Cromwell was said to have flung ink about, blotting the faces of his friends and having his own blotted in turn.

'Not that I'd ever believe such wicked lies about the master,' Polly had stated loudly, her face turning crimson on seeing Frances standing at the kitchen door, her every word overheard. 'It's a crying shame, a good man like that – a good Christian Puritan – being lied about as indulging in such wicked play as a schoolboy would have been whipped from here to kingdom come for. Never would I ever believe such tales of a good, kind and upright man.'

Frances had felt that Polly had been overdoing her loyalties a little as she blustered on, 'What I say is it's them Royalist sympathisers as is putting around such tales. The streets abound with spies for all the Army routs them out.' All of this said to a return to scrubbing the pots in the washing bowl with a burst of energy she rarely showed if not urged on by Pearson.

Anger had wrung Frances' heart, as it did now, that her father could be so hated. He was indeed stern and unbending, but to her he was a kind and loving father and had never in his whole life raised his voice much less his hand to his 'little wenches', as he fondly called her and Mary.

'I sorely miss Papa today,' she hissed, needing to talk to help along this tedious sojourn they were being compelled to keep. 'I wish I knew how he is faring. It is said he laboured long on this dreadful matter. Perhaps even now the King will be spared.'

'I doubt it,' said Mary, unable to resist a reply. 'Papa may be slow in making up his mind, but once he has, nothing will alter it.' It was her turn to cast a wary glance at her mother as another page of the bible was turned. 'Anyway, what do you know about it? You're still a child.'

'And you're not!' challenged Frances a little too loudly.

At the warning click of their parent's tongue, they each lowered their heads hastily, applying themselves to silent contemplation. But it couldn't last and soon Frances was restless again.

'We all know the King is bad.' Not that she understood the strife that had existed between king and parliament. All she knew was that civil war had raged as far back as her young years allowed her to remember, keeping her father from his family for long periods just when she began to need his companionship, loving him so. To her mind his absence was entirely the King's fault.

Sometimes in bed at night she would be filled with fear of Papa being killed in some skirmish. And not only him, but her brothers Henry and Dick, for hadn't Papa's favourite son Oliver been killed in battle with the King? And there were her older sisters' husbands – they too had been in the thick of it all. Not that she worried about what happened to Bridget's husband.

She didn't much like Henry Ireton – a thin fidgety man with narrow eyes and a tight mouth. How Bridget ever found pleasure in him was beyond her except that they were a pair well matched.

John Claypole, though, was a likeable person and Frances had just as great a fondness for him as she had for Betty. He had a kind, rounded face, full gentle lips and an infectious chuckle that drew everyone to him. The two were so alike, Betty with the same playful nature even though she suffered so much from those frequent pains in her stomach. How dreadful it would have been for her if John Claypole had been killed because a wilful king had wanted to rid himself of parliament and rule alone.

'He is the worst king . . .' she burst out impulsively,

rewarded by her mother's angered voice piercing the quiet of the room.

'I gave you good warning, Frances. Now to your room, miss. Remain there until you are bidden to return downstairs.'

'But Mama . . .' The bedrooms were freezing. No fires had been lit in them and the icy outside air would have seeped in through even the tiniest crevice.

'No!' came the adamant response. 'Your room shall give you the opportunity to reflect upon your impiety at this tragic time.'

True loving sister, Mary sprang to her assistance. 'Oh, please let her stay here in the warm, Mama. I swear she'll be good.'

Mrs Cromwell's plump face regained none of its usual composure. 'You hold yourself highly, miss, in your swearing. Frances will oblige us by doing as I ask of her and remain there until sent for. You will stay by me, Mary, then no mischief will be wrought.'

So there it was. The rest of the day spent in isolation, shivering under the bedcover. But it wasn't as bad as Frances had expected. Terribly cold of course, but huddled under the coverlet in a fit of pique at the injustice of it all, she began to warm up except for the tip of her nose, grateful that here there was no one to scold her for impiety. Not only that. On a small stand by the window was her embroidery.

Creeping out of bed she went and plucked out the needle, still with thread attached. Feeling deliciously wicked, she began to stitch a button of apple blossom on a leafy bough.

Below the window, more people were passing, heading for Whitehall. Embroidery forgotten, she opened the casement window, quietly lest it be heard downstairs. The icy air slapped at her cheeks, bearing with it the distant murmur of what she guessed had to be hundreds of people. She remained leaning out, listening, picturing the scene – the waiting crowd, the scaffold, the black-draped block, the tall flat windows of the Palace of Whitehall, one window opening directly on to the place of execution and from which the King would emerge. A small, dignified man, she recalled, having seen him on one occasion.

Something, a subtle change in the tone of the distant throng, made her sure he had appeared. Automatically she tensed, leaning even further out to catch the triumphant howl of the spectators when the head of Charles finally rolled on to the sawdust. Instead, after all her waiting, all she heard was something that sounded like a groan or a profound sigh, as of a breeze moving through trees, springing up suddenly to fade away into the distance.

Was that all? Today a king had been beheaded. Parliament would not rule wisely, justly. Yet leaning from her window, expecting change, she could detect nothing. Almost as though nothing at all particularly unusual had occurred.

Vaguely disappointed, she closed the window gently, going back to her embroidery while below her people moved in silent groups, homeward.

'Mother says you may come down to supper.' Mary poked her head around the door to the bedroom she and Frances shared.

Frances, surprised to find it dark, squinted at the light from the candle Mary was holding. 'I must have fallen asleep,' she said, sitting up. 'Is it late?'

'Not too late for supper. There's mutton stew, and mother says you must come down as she will be reading the Bible to us afterwards. She says you are in great need of it.' There was laughter in Mary's voice.

It had hardly been worthwhile getting up. Supper over,

engrossed in listening to their mother, in no time at all it was bedtime, but their father hadn't returned home. She and Mary lay awake for some time talking over the day's events.

'I can hardly believe the King is dead,' Mary finally yawned and turned over in the bed they shared, her actions denoting an end to talk and time for sleep.

Frances lay awake still. She heard the creak of the stairs as her sisters made their way up, the light of their candle glinting briefly through the chinks in the door. She had meant to stay awake to listen for Papa coming home, aware that she had fallen asleep only when voices downstairs brought her back to her senses. One was her mother's, but that other, though muffled by the floorboards, wasn't the slightly nasal, penetrating tone of her father.

Gripped by curiosity, she crept out of bed. Her first thought had been to wake Mary, but two of them might alert the speakers to eavesdroppers, so she tiptoed alone to the door, easing it open, and stepped out on to the small gallery at the head of the stairs.

Candlelight glowed from the open door of the parlour. By leaning over the balustrade, she could see the table, part of the hearth and her mother withdrawing a heated poker from the embers to dip into a pewter pot of ale which she handed to her visitor. By his buff uniform he was a young trooper; his tall metal helmet held in one hand out of respect for the lady's house, he accepted the pot in the other. His burnished breastplate had misted from the warmth of the room after the biting cold outside.

'Mulled ale will allay the night chill,' her mother was saying as the trooper took a deep draught. 'I am most grateful for your coming to reassure me, Sir, though my husband's need to remain at Whitehall was expected.'

The soldier was staring down at his ale pot. 'Ay, he appears to be filled with dolefulness, madam. Woefully grieved, strange to say, considering the personage whom this day . . . By your leave, Lady, I would relate a strange occurrence I witnessed as the small hours came upon us.'

Crouching behind the balustrade, Frances shivered with the cold. The man's remark had established it to be well past midnight.

'I was standing guard,' continued the man, 'in the room where the King's body had been placed for the night, the head by then reunited with the body . . .'

'Oh, pray, sir!' Her mother sounded distressed and the man was instantly apologetic.

'Madam, forgive my insensitivity.'

'Do continue, sir,' came her mother's voice a little sharply.

Clearing his throat, he put the ale pot on the table. 'Well, as I was saying, as I stood guard – and the Earl of Southampton will bear out my story, for he too was keeping vigil – about one of the clock the door opened, very stealthily, and we saw a heavily cloaked figure enter, his face muffled and his hat pulled down over his eyes. At first I thought it a ghost. Both the Earl and his companion started up, hands on swords, thinking it an intruder, but the figure raised a hand to bid them stay their swords – all this without a word spoken. As we watched, he moved to the coffin and stood gazing down at the corpse. Like a spectre he was, madam, so cloaked that none could've recognised him. But as he stood there, so solemn, I heard him mutter, "Cruel necessity." I swear it was the Lieutenant General hisself. Then he departed the room as silently as he'd entered, and us a-watching could make no move to ask any question of him, so sad was his presence and his leaving.'

'For a certainty it was my husband,' Frances heard her mother say. 'It is his nature to be compassionate, which in these difficult times must be well cloaked, as equally he had to cloak his identity in expressing his sorrow of a deed that had to be done.'

The trooper sounded ill at ease. 'I did feel it my moral duty to relate to you what I'd seen lest you be aggrieved by wicked rumours that the Lieutenant General did rejoice in the King's death. His enemies have said he did laugh and play the clown at the signing of the death warrant. There was none of the clown in the man this night.'

'It may well be,' came the firm reply, 'that when such a prodigious edict falls on a man's shoulders, its immensity will out in false high spirits lest he shatter beneath a strain too hard to bear. A weakness of the flesh such as our blessed Lord understood. There is no vindictiveness in my husband but a stern quest for justice. I do thank you for your kind loyalty.'

Frances cringed back against the gallery wall as her mother came into the hall, her visitor following. A draught of freezing air rushed up the stairs to envelop her as the outer door was opened.

'I bid you goodnight, Corporal . . .'

'Bowtell, madam,' he offered as she paused.

'I bid you goodnight, Corporal Bowtell, and God's peace to you.'

As the door closed, a sense of guilt assailed Frances, not so much from her eavesdropping as from the sensations that had flooded through her at the sight of the handsome young corporal who could not have been more than eighteen or nineteen.

Where she should have been awed by the tale of her father, there had come the thought of how handsome the soldier had been, the smooth face possessing such expression of concern that her heart had quite turned over. His shoulders had been broad beneath the tan leather of his jerkin. His hips had been slim. His hands when he had drawn off his gloves to accept the ale had been so supple that she at eleven years old hadn't been prepared for the strange tingle that had swept through her body. It had at once thrilled and alarmed her.

Kneeling, silent as a little mouse in her hiding place, she'd pictured herself being drawn close by those hands, the wide generous mouth pressed against hers and shiver after delicious shiver had passed through her. Now she shivered at her own boldness even in imagining such things. Surely for one her age, she must be quite wicked. Some dreadful punishment would be reaped upon her. Yet she couldn't get the young soldier and his effect on her out of her mind as hastily she crept back into her room, eased herself back into bed beside her unsuspecting, sleeping sister.

Snuggling against her as much for safety as for warmth, Frances closed her eyes against whatever punishment her wicked thoughts might bring, and forgot to think about how her father fared as pictures presented themselves against her closed eyelids of a young soldier embracing her.

Two

As the coach rattled the last few miles of dry, rutted road towards Hursley, Frances could hardly contain her excitement.

Three months since King Charles' execution. The episode of the young trooper had taken nearly all that time to get over. She had spent days afterwards in turn fearful of what might happen to her for what she had felt to be wicked excitement and revelling in that sensation which struck her as uniquely mature. But slowly the feelings had diminished, except for the odd moment when a picture of the young trooper with his fine body and supple hands – especially his hands – flashed through her mind, making her shiver deliciously with that unnamed excitement she had first experienced.

She had wanted to tell Mall about it, but Mall would have laughed at her and gone to tell Mama. Mama would have looked askance at her, taken her aside and disciplined her – a quick whipping which only stung a little through her clothes, but much worse, admonishing her verbally, making her feel chastened and ashamed, a much more lasting effect.

Today, however, dreams of a young soldier were pushed aside. They were going to a wedding, the whole family. Her brother Richard marrying the pretty, fair-haired Dorothy, daughter of a close friend of Papa, Mr Richard Mayor. The wedding was to be at Hursley Church near Mr Mayor's home in Hampshire, the Great Lodge at Merdon.

Civil weddings had become customary with the rise of the Parliamentarians, and although this wedding would take place in church, it would be a simple affair with a plain minister and plain sermon, singing and ceremony and organ music done away with.

Frances smiled. What a handsome couple Dick and Doll would make. Papa had been well pleased with the match and had taken Doll to his heart. But who wouldn't? She was such a pleasant girl. Though to see the faces of those in this coach none would guess they were going to a joyous occasion – this final stretch of road had taken its toll.

They had left London well before dawn – five adults (she considered herself and Mall adults too), two small children and one babe all cramped into one tiny space. There had been brief stops to rest, change the horses, eat and refresh themselves. Now it was dusk, the rolling wooded hills of Hampshire bathed in that ethereal light which seems to linger on and on after a fine sunny day, as though the whole world was holding its breath.

Frances threw a disparaging glance at the others. How could they ignore such beauty? How could they be so forlorn? Bridget complaining at every jolt of the coach, Mama's lips had grown tighter, she complaining very little. But every now and again she would stretch her back as though her shoulders ached, as well they might with Mary having fallen asleep across her lap, causing her to sit in one position for hours.

Bridget's husband, Ireton, cloaked as always entirely in black but for his broad white collar, had hardly spoken a word the entire journey apart from addressing the coachman, ordering their meals or replying briefly to an occasional query from Mama, and of course to comfort

Bridget when she sighed in weariness, his voice deep but utterly toneless.

To herself and Mary he hadn't spoken at all, merely frowned if they giggled together. The disapproving mouth above a small triangular smudge of beard, the dark censorious eyes that made men squirm uncomfortably beneath their stare made Frances equally uncomfortable. She would rather he'd ridden in the saddle beside the coach as most men did, but Bridget had begged he travel inside to help her control their children – Henry aged three and Elizabeth of two, Jane still a babe in arms.

Surrounded by females, thought Frances with wicked glee, no wonder he had little time for conversation. Even so, she wished she could escape those eyes. She couldn't wait to be in the company of the rest of her family, whose brighter spirits would be a fine tonic after fifteen hours confined in one cramped, jolting space. She wished Dick were here.

Richard and his brother Henry as his groomsman had travelled ahead, taking lodgings in Hursley village. Knowing Dick's talent for merry-making, they would be well into their cups prior to the knot being tied.

Betty and John Claypole were coming directly from their home at Norborough in Northamptonshire with their two boys, the journey done in stages. Soon they'd all be meeting up. There'd be a gaggle of Papa's sisters with their bright chatter, the bride's people too said to be a cheerful crowd. Only one thing clouded her horizon. Papa had warned that he might well be absent and had already conveyed regrets to Mr Mayor saying that even a Lieutenant General's life wasn't his own. But surely Papa would never miss his own son's wedding.

'I hope Papa is able to be there,' Frances burst out, rewarded by the sight of Ireton's dark brows again knitting together.

Her mother's reply was heavy with fatigue. 'I very much doubt it, my dear. So many pressing duties prevent him.'

'But such a special day.' She ignored Ireton's dark stare just as she ignored Bridget's exasperated sigh. 'He can't miss that.'

Her mother's tone remained gentle. 'Your father is as much governed by office as the humblest soldier in his regiment.' The word 'soldier' brought back memories, delicious and alarming, but Mama was still speaking. 'Even more, for much depends heavily on him. There is Parliament's dissention over the Irish question. There is Mr Lilburne and his Levellers stirring up trouble, demanding religious liberty and an end to military rule. To think what your father did for that man, keeping him from imprisonment, and this is how he shows his gratitude, by raising more discontent.'

Everyone knew of the man's recent incitement of an entire regiment to riot so that her father as Commander-in-Chief of the Army had been sent to quell it. Five of the ringleaders had been found guilty at a court martial. Ireton, true to form, had been all for executing the lot. But Papa had shown mercy, pardoning all but one, compelled at least to make an example. Frances had heard Mama talking about it to Bridget. 'Pardoning them all would have called into question his authority over the Army,' she had said. 'Men will ever mistake mercy for weakness, more's the pity.'

Trooper Robert Lockier, a soldier of seven years' loyal service, having been selected to face the firing squad in St Paul's Churchyard, the matter should have ended there. But Lilburne's followers had other ideas. Frances heard the tale from Pearson, the cook.

'A fine funeral they gave him. Trumpets sounding, and the Soldier's Knell being rung, loud enough for all London to hear. His horse following, all draped in black mourning cloth and attended by hundreds of them Sea-Green Men, as them Levellers call theirselves from them green ribbons they wear in their hats. Like a royal funeral it was. Thousands walking in rank and file. Your poor papa must truly think the whole country condemns his deed. Yet he was only doing what had to be done. We can't have the Army rioting, can we?'

But all this repercussion could mean Papa being kept from his own son's wedding.

'He ought to be allowed this one day,' she said heatedly. 'It isn't fair!'

'What a selfish child you are,' Bridget cut her short. 'In the first place, were he allowed to do as he pleased, he would first visit his mother, so old and frail has she grown. Dick is young and full of health while that old lady has but a year or two left to her.'

Frances glared at her across the dim interior of the coach. 'You've no care for Papa and even less for Dick. All you care—'

'What a wicked thing to say!'

Bridget's voice came shrill, her sharp face pinched with anger. In her arms Jane began to cry, prompting Ireton's intervention.

'My dear, control yourself. This isn't the time to bicker. We are tired.'

'And rightly said,' Elizabeth Cromwell began, but broke off with a small cry as the wheel struck a pothole. Her eyes sought Ireton's. 'Sir, I beseech you, command the driver to have more care for the womenfolk here. We are fair knocked to pieces.'

The pace moderating at his command, she breathed a sigh of relief. Mary, disturbed by the raised voices and the vehicle's dangerous lurch, sat up and rubbed her eyes, bewildered by finding it dusk.

'Where are we? Are we nearly there?'

'Not too far now.' Her mother's reply sounded like a thankful prayer.

Gently smoothing the chestnut hair as though Mary were a child, she regarded the others; Bridget's cheeks still flaring with indignation, Ireton's eyebrows drawn down still, and the pretty looks of her youngest daughter spoiled by stubbornness.

'It has been a long and tiresome journey,' she said quietly. 'We have endured it admirably so far, thank the dear Lord. Let's not fall to quarrelling at this final stage of it.'

She lifted a hand against an angry defence from Bridget. 'Bad enough the quarrels outside our family, your poor father not knowing where to turn to escape them. Should he arrive tomorrow, let him not find us also at odds with each other. Let us be in harmony for his sake at least.'

Mellowing a little, Bridget inclined her head. 'And pray the good Lord guide him and make him strong in all his decisions should there be any more uprisings.'

'Amen,' murmured her mother.

Ireton's voice came out of the gloom. 'Such demonstrations will not be repeated without dire punishment. Our Lieutenant General will not be so lenient next time. I shall see to that. He will bring the Army into line. And then, in full strength, we will go into Ireland. We will bring every Papist rebel of that heathen land to his knees or slaughter every last man, woman and child. In a sea of their own blood if need be.'

Frances saw her mother wince, but Mama said nothing. It was the most Ireton had said over the entire journey and its effect was to silence any further conversation for the rest of it.

The lamps of a coach were being extinguished as they finally turned into the courtyard of Great Lodge. The horses being unharnessed to be led away to the stabling yard showed that the coach had not long arrived.

'That must be Betty's,' Frances cried excitedly. Without waiting for aid she jumped down, the others being helped by Ireton, who handed each sleepy child into the care of waiting nursemaids while servants hurried to take down the travelling boxes.

'I was never so glad to arrive anywhere,' sighed Bridget. 'I vow Betty travelled in more comfort than we have.'

Candlelight glowed from every window of the fine manor as the party made their way from the coach to the house to be conducted in through the main entrance to a golden glow of welcome from the bride's mother.

Full-bosomed, fair hair in a frizzed topknot with some of it falling in ringlets on either side of her face, she presented a somewhat fluffy-minded woman even to the mass of lace at the cuffs and collar of her rose silk dress, far too high-waisted for a woman of her proportions.

She should be wearing a stomacher, thought Frances as Mrs Mayor practically launched herself at Mama. 'My dear Mrs Cromwell, you must be quite exhausted.'

'We are indeed,' Elizabeth smiled wanly.

'And Colonel Ireton.' She bobbed a small formal curtsy and stepped aside for him to usher his family into the oak-beamed hall. 'Mrs Ireton.'

Servants taking their outdoor clothes, Frances was overjoyed to see John Claypole come down the staircase towards them, evidence of Betty's arrival.

'She has retired,' he explained to her mother's enquiry as Mrs Mayor conducted them all into the panelled reception room. 'The journey brought on a most miserable stomach pain.'

Elizabeth's face lengthened in concern. 'Her father is ever begging her to pay more regard to her health. Her high spirits trouble him.'

Claypole nodded. 'She is wonderfully able to mask her discomfort. Your husband is right, dear Madam, she is too impetuous for her own good, but she does insist on waving away this weakness of the stomach.'

Frances watched her mother pat his arm. Mama displayed a great liking for him. Betty had been sixteen and he twenty-three when they had married. That had been four years ago and he had proved a sweet-natured husband, though maybe too indulgent of Betty's excitable disposition. Had he been more like Ireton, Frances thought, Betty's life would have been miserable to the extreme. As things were, she was ecstatically happy with a husband whose gentleness towards her was apparent to all.

Of slightly fleshy build, he had soft brown eyes, a hovering smile; his brows slanting up each side of his nose gave him the look of a dreamer and an artist. Indeed he was, as an architect, a man of construction rather than destruction, by no means measuring up to his father-in-law's hope of making a military man of him. Yet even Papa said he could not but help liking the man.

'You must not be too troubled over Betty,' her mother was saying. 'I think she has more resilience than we give her credit for.'

After a supper of cold meats, hot pease pudding, honey cakes and beer in convivial company of other guests, the womenfolk retired, leaving the men to their sherry sack and serious conversation.

Frances and Mary had been given a room at the top of the house. Sparsely furnished with two truckle-beds and a linen closet, a low fire nevertheless made the room cosy. After a maid had run a warming pan between the sheets, they were soon snuggled down, grateful to be there after their long journey yet still with heads too full to fall asleep.

'Do you wonder what newly-weds do, Frankie?' Mary mused.

She was sitting up, knees drawn up under her chin, arms clasped about them as she gazed pensively into the fire, it and the candle casting shadows across her pretty face.

Frances, lying flat with the covers drawn well up, didn't answer at once. The question had again taken her thoughts back to the night of the young trooper's call upon her mother.

'I've never given it thought,' she said finally.

Mary turned a taunting face to her. 'Oh come, Frankie, how can you say you've never thought at all about what they do?'

'I never have!' She felt suddenly hot with shame, expected to imagine her brother and his new wife in bed together. A sideways glance at Mall showed her still smiling.

'You'll be a woman yourself before long, Frankie. Surely you're having woman's curiosity – how it must feel to have a man's arms about you, a man embracing you, kissing you . . .'

'Oh, be quiet, Mall!' She turned away from the wise smile. 'We're too young to have such ideas.'

Mary giggled. 'Too young? Why, Betty was only three years older than I am now when she married. Daughters of poor men wed even younger. There's nothing sinful in dreaming of love. I can't believe you don't already. You are growing so swiftly. Before long you'll be having your terms. Even your bubs are beginning to show. Almost as noticeable as mine – see.'

Frances turned her head as Mary unlaced her nightgown to reveal the up-thrusting of tiny breasts tipped by pink, pouting nipples. She wrinkled her face into an exasperated expression.

'Oh, do cover yourself, Mall. I've no wish to see your bubs.'

Mary's taunting smile vanished. In sudden pique she re-laced her nightgown. 'You're being tiresome. Anyone would think there was a man in the room.' Leaning over to blow out the candle, she bounced down beneath the covers. 'Goodnight!'

Turning over, Frances closed her eyes tightly, she angry also. In the adjoining room children were giggling. From across the corridor came the low languid drone of women's voices conversing prior to falling asleep. From below she could hear men's muffled laughter. Somewhere outside the window a nightingale was trilling and warbling soft fluid notes. Gradually they became joined by the liquid tones of a soldier in buff uniform as he led her through a green wood beside a trickling stream. She felt the water lap deliciously against her bare flesh, cool against her skin, cool as his hands rested upon her budding breasts that had somehow become quite voluptuous . . .

Hursley Church, like many, had been stripped of all statuary and other items of idolatry. Walls had been stripped of pictures. The chancel no longer had a screen. The altar and choir stalls, even the crucifix, had been removed. An unnecessary instrument in the true worship of God. Only the pulpit remained.

Before a plain table stood the couple and before them the minister, in raven black from buckled shoes to tall-crowned hat, a wide white collar the only relief. He had assumed an air of expectancy, delaying the joining together of this couple, his eyes turning again and again to the church door. But Frances knew now that there would be no last-minute arrival.

To hide her bitter disappointment of Papa's non-appearance, she trained her eyes on the happy pair.

Dorothy's cream satin dress, its collar forming a wide cape, had green velvet sleeve panels and a deep matching hem stitched with gold thread and pearls. A demure dress in keeping with her nature. Pearls too adorned her abundant topknot and hung like raindrops in her side ringlets. Yet the adornment was nowhere overdone.

Frances could hear Papa's words in her head: 'I pray to the Lord she'll be a strength to Dick. Truly what my shallow gallant of a son needs.'

For all she missed him today, Frances felt a little sad at the way he regarded her favourite brother. It wasn't Dick's fault that he didn't take after him in the way Henry did. In fact he was so unlike his father as to seem not his son at all: a fine delicate face where Papa's was blunt and florid; gentle brown eyes where his father's were steely blue – eyes perfect to command men. And where Papa's hair was sparse and dusty, certainly no crowning glory, Dick's fell to his shoulders in a thick, glossy, tawny mane. Nor did Papa have any interest in clothes, wearing any old thing of sombre hue that happened to be near to hand. Dick chose his with deliberation, bright colours and rich cloth. Little of the Puritan about Dick. In cherry-red velvet, short tasselled jacket and breeches caught with gold ribbons above bucket boots of softest leather with turned-down tops, he'd have passed for a Royalist. Papa would have a fit were he here to see him.

He was ever lamenting what he called Dick's shortcomings, and she had to admit she could in a way see his side of it. No one could have tried harder to make something of him. He had even got him admitted to the Lincoln's Inn Society to study law, yet Dick had frittered away his time there in social pursuits, taking no interest in the civil wars. While Papa had been engaged in bitter conflict with the King, Dick was said to have had Cavaliers for companions and had even drunk the King's health with them. When Charles had been condemned to execution, Dick had dramatically flung himself at Papa's feet, pleading the King's cause. Oddly, Papa hadn't been unduly disturbed by such a disgraceful scene but Mama had been upset.

'To see my son in tears before all,' she had lamented, 'and his father a prospective leader of this country, too.' But Papa had dismissed her anger with that explosive, flat laugh of his. Odd, Frances mused as she saw the minister eyeing the church door yet again, how her father could so spoil his loved ones yet be so intolerant of others.

Her reverie came to an abrupt end with the clatter of hooves on the cobbles outside the church. Her heart gave a leap. She glanced at Mary.

'It's Papa!'

Moments later the big oak door opened slowly, its creaking echoing off the bare walls. There stood the Lieutenant General, his buff uniform and high-crowned, broad-brimmed hat powdered with dust, his features even more florid from his hard ride.

With him were an Army sergeant and a chaplain. His chaplains were mostly older, compelling men like the dour John Owen or the fiery-tongued Hugh Peter. But Frances noted that this was a young man, handsome even, despite his minister's black. He had the look of the gallant about him that plucked her eyes totally away from the entrance of her father.

The congregation's attention on him, Cromwell nodded briefly to his sergeant to withdraw, the door creaking closed, while Cromwell tiptoed down the nave trying not to acknowledge the grins that greeted his efforts.

His chaplain retired to the rear of the church, Cromwell finally and with a few audible grunts of apology got himself into the vacant place his wife had kept for him. There, the commander once more, he signalled to the minister to begin.

Fondness for him surged through Frances, for that gauche entrance rather than his normal command of self. It was said that he had merely to turn his gaze upon a man for that man to know himself under command. It was said that those eyes could peer into a man's very soul; that they could blaze with fanatical fervour and righteous anger. Yet Frances had never seen him angry with any member of his family, not even with Richard. Rather his eyes would become saddened by anything done amiss and perhaps that was harder to bear. His enemies may have spoken scathingly of his grim leadership, but towards his little wenches he was never anything but gentle, and when the occasion called, even merry.

It hurt her to hear his florid hue mocked, his nose described as monstrous, a delight taken in the proneness of his face to the occasional abscess. He was lampooned in London broadsheets for his notorious laxity of dress or care in shaving. It was these very things which made him dear to her – that her father was as vulnerable to small weaknesses as the next man. Quite suddenly her heart flowed out to him.

'Oh, I do love you, Papa!' she burst out as the minister was about to speak. The next instant she was hanging her head in shame as a ripple of laughter ran around the congregation.

The day had smiled on the newly-weds. A cloudless sky, a day as warm as high summer, the air perfumed by the scent of spring flowers and new green buds. Dorothy's delphinium-blue eyes had strayed again and again to her new husband as she received their guests' best wishes for her happiness, Richard's own gaze following her adoringly as a little dog would its mistress.

Seeing them, Frances found herself envious, though why, she wasn't sure. She knew a sense of loneliness was building up inside her. She felt strangely at odds with this happy gathering. She felt ignored. Yet rather than pull herself out of her apathy there was a morbid desire to extend it, and when Mary asked her to play hide-and-seek with some of the younger children, she churlishly declined and wandered away among the chattering knots of guests.

Even her father, talking with a plump woman dressed in blue and cerise, his expression fixed with politeness as she extolled the virtues of her niece, the bride, could not lessen her mood when she came up to him and he put an arm about her waist.

'And what of my little wench?' he queried after introducing her to the woman and all those around him as 'the most charming of my daughters'.

Frances produced a broad smile for his benefit. 'Everyone is so very pleased you could be with us today, Papa.'

'Well said!' he exclaimed, beaming as everyone clapped their polite approval. Chuckling, he made a great thing of gazing about him, his rasping voice raised. 'Indeed, a most splendid occasion. And such a great wealth of colour from the ladies I see about me, and indeed some of the gentlemen – satin, velvet, frills, ribbons. Do I have *Royalists* at my son's wedding, I begin to wonder?'

The jest was greeted with laughter, but Frances remained sombre. 'Will you be returning to London with us, Papa?'

She saw his merriment fade. He lowered his tone. 'I fear not, little one.' He still persisted in calling her his little one although she reached nearly to his height, tall for her age. He had noted her pout, adding, 'I must visit your grandmother, and then on to duties that have greater claim on me at this time than my leisure. But I shall be with you all again soon.'

His arm slipped from her waist as yet another guest

claimed his attention and Frances moved away once more despondent. The Great Lodge was alive with chatter, with laughter, and colour, as her father had already remarked. Only a few here today had observed Parliamentarian sobriety, one of them of course Bridget, she in drab brown silk, and Mama, in quiet dove grey.

Betty, revived after a night's sleep, looked beautiful in green with gold appliqué around the hem, gold tassels and ribbons at her bare shoulders upon which her dark ringlets fell. Her brother Henry looked splendid too, hardly less colourful than the groom, his russet velvet suit of the highest fashion with tassels at the edges of his jacket and knee breeches. Papa was right, they did all look like Royalists. Her own gown of hyacinth blue with a wide cape sewn with silver thread made her look very pretty, she observed in passing a mirror, but still did little to lift her spirits as she went into the garden with little else better to do.

Mary was on the lawn playing with Mr Mayor's two greyhounds. Seeing her sister she called for her to join her and for a while they both raced and squealed, the bounding dogs chasing them. But when Mary went back into the house for a cooling drink, Frances' mood swung back to melancholy and she wandered off, again wanting to wallow in herself.

Away from the house it was quiet, peaceful. The glow of the sinking sun behind groves of young elms reflected on tiny pink clouds suspended in a wash of translucent green was beautiful, lending a magic aspect to the vast grounds.

She followed a path bordered by a low box hedge, lavender and balm. It ended at a circular brick-paved area with a sundial and a stone bench. Sinking down on the bench, she rested her hands in her lap and gazed back at the house. Lamps were being lit. Guests were strolling on the terrace. She watched one figure detach itself from the rest to begin taking the path she had taken. Drawing nearer, she recognised it as that of the young chaplain who had accompanied her father. Frances felt her interest quicken.

He had obviously seen her from a distance, his approach purposeful, and reaching her he gave a small bow.

'Miss Cromwell?'

The slight lift of the corners of his lips could have been merely from politeness but his dark eyes regarded her with such appraisal that she was aware of feeling strangely self-conscious, that her heart had begun beating faster and her cheeks were glowing. She found herself taking in the attributes of the man: the high cheekbones, their healthy glow telling of an outdoor life rather than a cloistered one; the dark brown hair falling heavily to his fine shoulders while shorter strands lay in wayward fashion on his forehead. She became uncharacteristically flustered.

'Sir?' she countered, managing to control herself enough to incline her head in social greeting. But one of her ringlets fell forward and she saw his eyes flicker towards the movement. It had the result of sending a rush of blood to her cheeks to make her flush deeper and she quickly gazed down at her hands. He was staring at her far too boldly.

'You have me at a disadvantage, sir,' she hurried on, hoping to sound adult and lofty. After all, she was the daughter of his master and he was only his junior chaplain.

There came an apologetic intake of breath drawn in between closed lips. Looking up, Frances expected to see the apology reflected on his face. Instead she saw a now amused smile. He bowed with a deep flourish – to her mind also done with amusement.

'Forgive me, Miss Cromwell. I regret there is no one here to introduce us formally, which is a great pity. It appears I must take the initiative and introduce myself.'

His smile, however, was infectious and she found herself smiling back at him. 'Must you now?' she quipped lightly, feeling much easier.

Again the exaggerated bow. 'Jeremiah White at your service, Miss Cromwell. A very junior chaplain of your father.'

'I gathered that, Mr White,' she replied, her smile refusing to be controlled. 'But why have you sought me out so deliberately? As you see I am alone and would have thought you more prudent than to choose such a lonely place to acquaint yourself with a . . .'

She let her words fade, about to say defenceless woman, but to one at least ten years her senior she must seem a child, even though the woman within her fluttered and trembled.

He didn't seem to notice her hesitation but his face grew serious. 'Ah, there was a purpose. Your father charged me to bring you back to the house as it is growing dark, and also he is about to take his leave.'

Consternation gripped at her, not only at her father leaving. 'Shall you be accompanying him?' she heard herself asking.

'I am afraid so.'

Frances drew in a deep breath and stood up quickly to control the feelings that surged through her. The stone seat had begun to feel cold. The air had grown chill.

'Then I best go bid my father farewell,' she said firmly, and moving off was very conscious of the young chaplain following politely a few paces behind.

Going early to bed after Papa and Mr White had left, Frances hadn't waited for Mary, needing to be alone to relive that walk back to the house.

The air at dusk had carried a fragrance that still lingered in her mind. Mr White had caught her up after a while to present his arm for her to hold. 'Lest you fall, Miss Cromwell.' His voice had been soft. 'It is quite dark and the path is uneven.'

The warmth of his arm had penetrated the sleeve of his black cleric's coat, the sensation bringing little knots of pleasure to her stomach. Casting a furtive glance at the finely chiselled features she had debated his age. Twenty-two perhaps. By the time she was ready for marriage in three or four years, he still might not be too old for her. Young women did marry older men.

Lying there with time to reflect, she chided herself for thinking such fanciful rubbish. He'd been oblivious to her proximity as he related bits of his life as her father's chaplain. And yet as they reached the periphery of the glow from the house windows, he had paused to look directly at her, his eyes just a little above hers and for a moment she saw herself through those eyes, the woman he had seen in her, that for all her having only just reached the age of twelve she possessed a certain maturity; something in his gaze told her that he was contemplating the woman she was to become.

In taking leave of her, he had taken her hand and put it to his lips and had expressed the hope that his duties would bring him into her presence again. When that would be, there was no way of knowing, but what she did know was that she would be a little older by then and it wouldn't be only Papa she would be watching for.

Three

Closeted from the world by the drawn bed curtains of crimson damask, Dorothy lay in the crook of her husband's arm, gazing up into his face.

'I am the most fortunate woman in the world with the most handsome husband and a beautiful home. What more could any girl wish for?'

Her father had given the house as part of her dowry. On the edge of Hursley village, its leaded windows peeped out from under a thatched roof towards a fine parcel of land and, beyond, the serenity of the Hampshire downs.

Richard gazed down at her. 'And I have myself a sweet and beautiful and loving wife, so surely my fortune is as great as yours.'

'Then we are indeed a fortunate pair,' she giggled as he leaned over her and lightly kissed her lips.

'And we shall live here in complete luxury the rest of our lives.'

Again she giggled. 'What will you do, pray, to keep us in luxury?'

'Become a soldier like my father. Become a great general though it will take me away from you for months on end.'

Her alarm was immediate. She pulled away from him. 'Oh, no! Dick, how could I survive without you?'

Laughing, he toppled her on to her back, leaning over

her to hold her prisoner. 'I'm teasing, my heart. I would never leave you, as my father so easily leaves his wife. No, my dearest, I concede the glory to him and my brother Henry. My sweet Doll, I shall never desert you, never.'

Relaxing his hold on her, he lay back, his tone growing thoughtful.

'My sole ambition is to be a farmer, a country squire like your father. And everyone in Hursley will offer me their respect and admiration.'

So she would not be left here alone. Dorothy gave a little laugh, her mood lightening.

'Your *sole* ambition, my lord?' she hinted impishly. She saw him give a knowing grin, but the grin faded and he became pensive again.

'My father once farmed. Huntingdonshire, and after that, St Ives in Cambridgeshire. He was a Member of Parliament but he loved farming more. He loves horses and hunting. He once even considered emigrating to the Americas, but he became dragged ever deeper into politics, which now claims his whole time. It has taken a toll on him dreadfully. I knew him when he'd be merry the whole day, but now . . . I'll not let that happen to me. I shall be a country squire and have all my troubles seep through my fingers into the soil.'

'What troubles do you anticipate, darling?' she asked, but his mind wasn't on her.

'We'll sow the arable land your father has given us and graze cattle on the rest. It'll take a goodly sum to start off, but I can always borrow. Once the harvest comes in it will all be paid back. It is a little too late to sow now, but cattle fattened for the winter will bring a good price and by next spring we will be in funds.'

'But you know little about farming.'

'I shall learn. Your father will help me, advising me and such, will he not?'

But Dorothy had lost interest in farming. A surge of love for Richard making her unusually bold, she turned towards him, and seeing his chest bared by the unlaced nightgown, began playfully to nibble at the fine hair she discovered there. With her fingers she began to trace where her teeth had touched, a gentle exploration now delighting in those realms unknown to her until a moment or two ago. She made her tone enticing.

'And what field will you plough first?' But he was already aware of her purpose even as she added, 'A farmer must sow—'

'That we can remedy,' he broke in. 'They say every journey begins with the first step.'

Moving to lie over her, his hands began to caress her gently, then more urgently until, shy as she had been, she cried out for him. Soon he was guiding himself into her, she breathless with new wonder and awe of the sensations he aroused.

That night Dorothy conceived his child, but an excited and wild ride up to Merton Castle with him the following month, resulting in a trifling tumble from her mare which had seen them both laughing as he helped her to her feet, put an end to the tiny spark of life within her a few weeks later.

She was disappointed, of course, but not unduly upset. She was young and healthy. She had her whole life ahead of her and a month or two after that found herself pregnant again. Her letter to her husband's parents telling of her little loss brought a casual observation from her mother-in-law with the knowledge of one who had suffered many a miscarriage in her life. 'She will bear others,' she said, not unkindly. 'She is yet young.'

Oliver was much more touched, disappointed that his new daughter-in-law would not make him a grandfather just yet.

'I shall write her a tender letter of condolence,' he vowed. 'The first moment I am allowed a little time to do so. Perhaps later this week.'

It was to be longer than that, as more trouble with the Army took him off yet again, Ireton's regiment at Salisbury refusing to go to Ireland until it received settlement of its pay arrears.

'It's that detestable Mr Lilburne stirring up unrest again,' Frances heard her mother complaining to her other daughters on one of their social visits. 'You would think he would learn, having been imprisoned before for the same treason. Now your father and General Fairfax must go to quell the mutiny that awful man has provoked.'

Frances knew how she felt about these enforced absences. She too was finding herself longing for someone whose absence had made him all the more precious to her as she sat dreaming about her father's handsome young chaplain, Mr Jeremiah White.

Common sense told her to harden herself against wishful thinking, that he must have forgotten her. Anyway, what would he want with one as young as her? But longing was no respecter of age and refused to be banished by common sense. How she hated this feeling of hopelessness. But the following week her mother was again happy.

'Your father has managed to procure some ten thousand pounds from under the very nose of Sir Harry Vane of the Admiralty. It was destined for the Navy and he was very put out by the ruse, being already at odds with your father. But at least the Army will be paid and your father will soon be home.'

And his junior chaplain too, came the excited thought. Frances found herself daring to conjecture that perhaps she and Mr White would renew their acquaintance. She began planning what to wear for when they met, how best to look, how to behave more adult before him, even practising each time she was alone. But it didn't happen.

Within days, a regiment led by a Captain Thompson ignored the pay settlement and joined the mutineers of Ireton's regiment. Cromwell set out after them immediately, and at Bursford village in Oxfordshire overpowered them as they slept. Some were killed, hundreds more imprisoned – crammed into the church for nearly a week – and three of the ringleaders executed.

'It isn't fair,' Frances railed to her mother. 'Everything is put against Papa coming home.'

'I know you miss him,' her mother commiserated, then brightened up. 'Parliament is hailing him as a hero, and you must not begrudge him that. He'll be home before you know it, Frankie.'

Frances found that little help. Parliament might hail him as a hero – the rest of the population didn't.

News of the incarceration and execution of Army personnel had not been at all well received. When Cromwell finally came home at the end of May with other military leaders to a banquet given by the City of London in his honour, he was met with jeers, and a linchpin craftily removed from his coach held up the whole procession amid exulted cheers at his expense.

'I think they're treating Papa horridly,' Betty moaned, but all Frances could think of was seeing Mr Jeremiah White entering at the heels of Papa, his dark eyes settling upon her.

But when Papa did come home, Mr White wasn't with him. She could hardly make her feelings obvious by asking after him. She did risk a casual enquiry or two, but Papa, being too occupied and tetchy to take account of it, left her wary of pressing him any further.

There was much to make him tetchy. Growing disunity in

Ireland, General George Monck barely holding on against sympathisers in league with Catholics such as Ormonde and Lord Inchiquin and rebels such as Owen O'Neill. Prince Rupert of the Rhine, a staunch ally of young Charles Stuart, was plaguing Ireland's southern coast. There was also the business of the assassination by Royalists of Doctor Dorislaus, the new envoy to Holland. All of London had been appalled, especially when the Dutch government had made little effort to bring the culprits to justice even though they knew who they were. Although a great funeral was held in London it caused a considerable rift between both countries.

All this had brought visitors to spend long hours with Frances' father, cooped up with him. Even Mama, having to arrange food and drink for them all, was becoming a little put out, long-suffering as she was.

'This house has become a tavern,' Frances heard her rail at him after another late-night visitor had departed.

It was well past midnight. King Street deserted. The street falling silent as the clatter of hooves on the damp cobbles faded away. Everyone had gone to bed, including Mrs Pearson, and even their new housemaid, Lettie, who had replaced the idle Polly. Frances lay awake, Mall sound asleep beside her, and listened to their mother's annoyed tones. Annoyed or not, her voice was not raised. She didn't need to. Her tone was always enough.

Frances strained her ears to hear what was being said, hopeful of the unlikely chance of catching any reference to Mr White, but of course his name did not come up and she finally fell asleep.

Oliver had sunk down upon the oak settle in the little parlour. He busied himself lighting his pipe of tobacco, surrendering himself to his wife's pique.

'I understand your weariness of the way this house is,'

he soothed as she moved back and forth. 'But it'll not be long now before we quit this place.'

Elizabeth stopped her irate pacing, her large, slightly drooping eyes focusing on him. 'Quit this place? If you mean this house, I am quite contented with the house. It is merely all the comings and goings of your endless visitors that plague me. I might well consider dismissing Lettie and taking her place, so much of a waiting maid have I become.'

A chuckle escaped him and a spark of playfulness pushed aside his weary expression. 'Then you have no interest in a grand house in Dublin?'

'Dublin?'

Patting the settle he bade her sit down. 'It has been finally agreed that Ireton and I depart for Ireland within the month.' Drawing on his pipe, he blew out an aromatic cloud of smoke, allowing time for his news to sink in as Elizabeth sat down beside him.

Placing his pipe on the rack in the empty hearth, he leaned towards her and patted her hand to ease her confusion.

'We all go together. The whole family. With the exception, of course, of Dick and his wife. Not long wed, they have more to interest them than military affairs. But you, my dear, will reside in a grand house in the most fashionable part of Dublin, and you will be my right hand and the hub of all in that city. It will be a longish stay while we put down Irish Royalists and Papists. By the way, our son Henry is to have the rank of Colonel. I am to be given the rank of Commander-in-Chief and Lord Lieutenant of Ireland. Although I have told Parliament that I am unworthy of such promotion they will have it so. So there it is, Elizabeth. What do you think of it?'

She did not reply for a moment, then finally she said

quietly, 'I think you must be both very pleased and honoured. Now I need my bed, dear.'

That was all she said, despite his trying to draw her out more. Nor did she refer to it again. But so wrapped up in his own excitement of the coming expedition, Oliver didn't once pause to wonder at her lack of it.

By the beginning of July the house was in a turmoil of preparation. Boxes and chests were stacked everywhere, Elizabeth insisting on taking every last bit of household linen as well as half her precious furniture, almost driving poor Lettie mad, who endured it all nevertheless. After all, going with them as lady's maid to the two younger Cromwell girls – that promotion as well as a higher salary more than compensated for this present upheaval. Having never been out of London in her life, much less out of the country, Lettie was a willing helper.

Frances took part in the preparations with mixed feelings. 'Will that new chaplain of Papa's, Mr White, be going with him? We've not seen the man since Dick's wedding.'

Fortunately her mother was so deep in the throes of packing that she missed the significance behind her daughter's question. Busy counting her linen boxes to be shipped off to Dublin, she didn't even look up.

'I cannot imagine your father having only one chaplain, Frankie. Every regiment has its own. With so many regiments going, they could well form a regiment of their own, I shouldn't wonder.'

'But will Mr White be one of them?' Frances dared to persist.

'Mr White? I've no idea, child. What a question!'

Frances felt a little too close to betraying herself. What if Mama began probing? She decided it better not to ask any more questions concerning Mr White.

*   *   *

It was developing into a last-minute rush. For weeks there had been endless argument over funds to equip the expedition. Her father having finally got permission to raise them from the City of London on the sale of Dean and Chapter lands and from pledges from the Royal Free Farms and Adventurers from Goldsmiths Hall, there was now nothing more to be done but look forward to Ireland.

'Have you seen this broadsheet?' Excitedly, Mary waved a copy of the *Mercurius Politicus* under Frances' nose as packing finished at last and supper lay on the table ready for them.

'It says Papa is to be paid *eighteen thousand* pounds a year. Even King Charles in his time could not have been so rich. Think of all the gowns we shall be able to buy!'

'Is that all you can think about?' Frances snapped. To her mind they were in danger of becoming too grand. Too grand perhaps for the services of a green young minister like Jeremiah White, her father surrounding himself with far more learned men. It seemed that her hope of ever seeing Mr White again could pop like a soap bubble.

Mary put the broadsheet on a chair and came to the supper table. 'What do you think Dublin will be like? They say the Irish are wild and unwashed, and most go barefoot like the urchins do in London. I do hear they've been known to eat Protestants. Tearing them to pieces. Like wolves.' She gave a shudder.

'You will find Dublin very English,' said her mother, the severity of her tone from the head of the small table warning Mary against such childish flights of fancy. 'The people there are Anglo-Irish and of strong Parliamentarian sympathies. And may I remind you, Mall, that I wish for none of your bloodthirsty speculations while we are at supper.'

Mary hung her head. Frances smirked. But as they eventually left the table ready for reading from the big bible, Mary muttered covertly, 'I bet they do too eat Protestants.'

The following evening, his artillery and ammunition shipped ahead of him, their father gave a grand farewell dinner party. But it was five days before he finally left on Wednesday the eleventh of July, and even that took ages with long speeches delivered by one dignitary after another, each trying to outdo the other in invoking God's blessings upon the venture.

Before the soporific droning of oration, Frances found herself hardly able to keep awake as she sat with her family beneath the awning of the rose-bedecked platform. Her father, not known for his brevity either, took a great time in addressing his well-wishers until the failing light of a mostly overcast day in the end forced him to depart. Every street packed with wildly cheering crowds, old scores forgotten, the Lord Lieutenant once more their hero, he left amid blaring trumpets and fluttering banners.

His own coach flying the white standard of peace, pulled by six white Flemish mares, and with a procession of over eighty officers of his Army, a brilliant setting sun broke through momentarily as though to add its own blessings on the occasion, almost like a wonderful omen, the crowds not slow in seeing it as such.

Frances had never felt so proud of him – of what he meant to this country. But her happiest sight was of several mounted chaplains together looking like a black smudge against the wash of red, buff and gold as they passed. Most were in their middle years, but among them one young face stood out. It was the briefest of glimpses, and he did not see her even though she cheered and waved so much that her mother had to lay a restraining hand on her arm.

'We follow tomorrow morning,' she said sternly, yet her smile was tolerant. 'You'll see your father soon enough when we reach Milford Haven.'

Frances sobered, watching the black-clad group ride out of sight. She'd be seeing Jeremiah White after all and she intended to make the most of it to make him notice her. Dublin was going to be wonderful.

Weary from days in slow freight wagons, the Cromwell family arrived to find Milford Haven – with five cavalry regiments and six infantry regiments as well as over a thousand dragoons – resembling more a garrison than the quiet Welsh sea town it would normally be. It was here that Cromwell had been awaiting further supplies of ammunition, food, clothing, and the hundred thousand pounds he had finally raised for this expedition.

'I've never seen so many troops together in one place,' whispered Mary as the travel-worn family toiled into the town. 'At least the shop people will be doing a good trade.'

True, every man, now in good heart, back-pay burning holes in his purse, plus three months' advance to spend or save as he wished which, from the way it was being spent, he mostly preferred to spend, crammed into every shop that caught his eye, and every woman who took his fancy.

Cromwell, quick to notice, grinned indulgently.

'It goes well for them now,' he remarked to Ireton over dinner in his quarters above the Boar Inn after seeing his family settled.

There was a gleam in Ireton's eye. 'They see nought but hunting the women at this moment. But we'll give 'em finer hunting when we reach Ireland. We'll blood 'em with Papist blood – that of every man, woman and child who hinders us.'

Cromwell gave a great belly-laugh as he cut himself

a generous portion off a huge and succulent joint of beef which an awed and bobbing serving wench had brought in.

'Have done now! We'll see blood enough, I don't doubt.' He became suddenly serious. 'But remember, Henry, where we go, there will go God. We will be as just and fair as he would have us be.'

Ireton was slicing a fastidiously small portion of the meat. Proceeding to cut it into neat, bite-sized pieces on his plate, he growled, surly, 'And if God is to be revenged for the vileness done to the good Protestants of Ireland these eight years back, would He not rejoice to see done to them that which they did to innocent families during the atrocities of the Papist plot? 'Did they not butcher every man, woman and child – slaughter and burn the babes before their mothers' very eyes?'

His knife cutting viciously into the juicy meat, it was as though he was cutting into each Irish rebel as he raged on, seemingly out of control. 'Did they not ravish married women and tender virgins alike, torture and kill their menfolk, then turn out what was left to starve, burning their crops and their homes? Would not God demand to be revenged of such vileness, even after eight years? Now we are being threatened with yet more violence. This time we will treat like for like.'

'That we will do,' said Cromwell, but more mildly, a little taken aback by the other's vehemence. Cutting his meat busily, he began chewing it in great lumps. 'But we should not proceed like animals, but as God Himself would wish us to. Aye, avenge those fearful deeds we will, with strength and resolve, but with justice too – for the innocent women, the innocent babes.'

'We shall see,' said Ireton, grim and determined as he picked daintily at a potato. 'When the time comes and we see those foul creatures face to face, then we shall see.'

* * *

It was the thirteenth of August before they finally embarked – a miserable day with rain in the gusty wind.

'I shan't be at all sorry to leave this place,' complained Bridget to her husband as she repacked the few things she had used for her stay. She and the family would follow two days after Cromwell and his troops had left.

'Our little Jane has had colic the whole time we have been here. As for myself, I have atrocious heartburn because of the tavern fare we've been forced to eat here, and I've yet to experience any comfortable bed. Surely our crossing can be no worse than our journey here.'

'Then I pray God gives you a smooth crossing,' said Ireton fervently.

She gazed at him, chewing her lips. 'Could it be then that it might be rough? I'm dreading it, Henry. I'm not a good traveller, as you know. Getting here was dreadful enough. The wagon with my mother's household goods broke down, adding almost a week to our journey. I can only give thanks to God that we weren't set on by robbers.'

'It was for that reason your father had some of his sturdiest troopers give you protection, with no other men about you.'

The remark made her immediately testy. 'My brother Richard came along to give us his protection,' she said, snatching a child's garment from the nurse she had brought with her for the children. She saw Ireton give a thin sneer.

'May God protect us all from your brother Richard's protection,' he muttered aphoristically, and left her to her packing.

Prior to sailing, Cromwell took them all down to view the ships lying in Milford Haven's deep sinuous channel.

'What d'you think of our proud fleet, my dear?' he asked his wife and heard her gasp in wonder.

'It's . . . it's a veritable armada.'

The channel, with its rock-fringed grassy slopes rising steeply from the water's edge, was a forest of swaying spars and masts in the gusting wind that had this morning arisen. Soon their sails would billow and fill and bear him away across that perilous stretch of sea to a hostile land.

'If I could only be at your side,' she fretted, the wind almost taking her bonnet from her head, her arm linked through his to steady herself.

'You will later, my dear,' he soothed. 'I regret I have no option other than to venture out upon these foaming waves, but the signs are that this wind will die in a day or two and your own crossing will be more pleasant.'

She clutched his arm even tighter. 'I hope you are not made ill by them, Oliver, and arrive without mishap. I shall pray constantly for your safety until I am able to join you.'

'And my prayers for yours,' he murmured, his hand on hers.

Elizabeth leaving to join the others gave him the opportunity to take his son to one side.

'I have meant to speak to you, Dick, of Doll's miscarriage. I regret I have not expressed my condolences earlier, but I urge you to ensure she take better care of herself. I need to stress the importance of it, as has been proved by her recent loss through carelessness.'

Knowing his father to make long speeches, Richard resigned himself to enduring this one, knowing that interrupting might only prolong it.

'This losing of a child so swiftly after begetting . . .' the tuneless voice continued. 'Her father, my dear friend, did write to me that a fall from her horse during a mad and foolish ride with you might have been the cause.'

He paused as two of his men came to collect his impedimenta to take on board. 'It was foolhardy of you, Dick, to allow her to take such risks with herself. Surely you were aware that she was pregnant.'

'It was too soon to know,' Richard defended, but was waved aside.

'You ought to have known. Newly wed – how other would she be after a few weeks married? You have always been foolhardy, Richard. However, I put this particular oversight down to the ignorance of a young husband. But I beg you, Richard, to urge her that she as a dutiful wife henceforth curb her high spirits lest a similar escapade rob her of motherhood yet again.'

'Very well, Father,' Richard obliged, but his silent sigh did not escape the man long able to detect mendacity in others well enough to thunder his indignation at them. Because Dick was his son, however, whom he loved dearly, he kept his voice low and steady.

'I'll not weary you, Dick,' he said sadly and pointedly. 'Sufficient that I remind you of your responsibilities as a husband, and Doll's as a mother to your children when the Lord sees fit to make her so. I shall write to her before I sail, and to her father also.'

Spoken to as though he were a child had not sat well with Richard and it was his sullenness that stopped him enlightening his father to Doll's present condition. His reason was twofold. To have told him mid-sentence in his splendid oration that she was pregnant again would have exacted an even lengthier tirade of advice, and that he wasn't prepared to endure. He was a married man now. He could take care of himself and Dorothy without help from Father. Also a certain bloody-mindedness had taken hold, the Devil whispering in his ear, 'Let him stew awhile. That will teach him!'

No one could have felt more relief when his father finally

stepped into the cockboat after having embraced him with special affection above the rest of the family.

True to his word, Oliver wrote to Dorothy the moment he was aboard, the letter brought to Richard by a messenger from the ship. It was sealed and bore only her name, that action alone making him all the more resentful.

His father must know that, like any good and loving wife, Doll would hand it to her husband to read. So why shut him out? But he had already guessed at its content – a virtual repetition of all he'd said on the quayside along with his condolences, urging her to bear her loss with fortitude, that she would be in his prayers for her well-being and not to despair but seek the Lord frequently and implore her husband to do likewise, and above all, conduct herself with more propriety befitting a married woman.

'Our lives are our own,' he grumbled to himself, and as the figure of his father appeared on deck to wave a loving farewell to them all to cheers from others watching, Richard bent his head and strode swiftly away.

Four

It was not two days but a week before the weather was finally gentle enough to allow Elizabeth and her daughters a smooth crossing.

She stepped ashore in Dublin to find that Oliver, with her son Henry, had already left for Drogheda thirty miles to the north. Ireton had sailed on with his thirty-seven vessels to land in the south. So once again both women were without their menfolk.

'How is my husband?' Elizabeth asked the dragoon assisting her on to dry land.

'Fully recovered, ma'am,' he said brightly. 'Back to good health once more.'

Startled, she let go the supporting hand and would have almost fallen backwards into the brown waters of the Liffey had he not caught her hand again and steadied her. 'Have a care, ma'am!'

She ignored the warning. 'Recovered? Are you saying he's been ill?'

'Not ill as such, ma'am.' She saw his lips quirk a little. 'The sea last week was choppy, to say the least.'

While speaking he was helping Bridget and her children ashore, then Frankie and Mall, one after the other, not paying Elizabeth that much attention now. Nor did she take kindly to that curl of his lips, as though ridiculing her husband. Seeing her looking at him, he quickly sobered.

'It made your husband fearful seasick, ma'am. The Irish Sea can affect even the most seasoned sailor. But it did not diminish him before our eyes one bit. He bore it stoically, better than did any of us.'

Her annoyance mellowing, her eyes became anxious. 'You say he has recovered completely?'

'No sooner had he set foot on dry land, Lady Cromwell, he was fully recovered.'

Elizabeth gave him a look. Still not used to this new form of address now that Oliver had been made Lord Lieutenant, a small suspicious streak in her nature made her instinctively search for hidden mockery when used. But there was only respect in the man's expression, together with obvious gratification in being the bearer of pleasing news regarding her husband's health.

'I'm glad to hear it,' she relented, and with her possessions now being piled up on the quayside she followed him as he led the way between a good crowd that had gathered to see the Cromwell ladies come ashore, some merely to gawk, but some with genuine welcome.

He had begun by striding ahead, but slowed to allow her to walk at his side. Resplendent in Venetian-red slashed sleeves, buff coat, black breeches, a crimson feather in his soft-brimmed hat, the mid-afternoon sun glinting off breast plate and gorget and the spurs of his bucket boots, he towered over her and Elizabeth found herself glad for the confidence his presence gave her before this crowd.

'Aye, Lady Cromwell,' he continued. The man was most certainly a blabberer. 'It is always so – laid low though a man might be by the rolling of a ship, it's all forgotten the instant he gets solid ground 'neath him. In truth, the Lord Lieutenant was so well recovered he was all for being off after them rebels in Drogheda that very day, and in full command. But he had to curb his impatience till all was unloaded and assembled ready. And that do take time, my lady. Thirty-five ships is no mean feat to unload.'

'I dare say,' agreed Elizabeth as they turned off on to a street. Their way was still all but blocked by a sea of faces beneath the overhanging upper storeys of the houses they passed, spectators readily parting for them with many a protracted 'aah' for Bridget's children, and a lilting 'Welcom-ter-Doblin-moi-laidy' for Elizabeth herself.

Frances and Mary in white lawn caps and lace shawls over dresses of dove grey and biscuit beige drew envious sighs from drab-skirted, brown-shawled women, accompanied by whispers of, 'the darrlin' darghters of the Lard Lieutenant himself'.

In a square not far off, carriages awaited them. Here stood a far more finely attired assembly ready with a preliminary welcome from the dignitaries of the town and their ladies. It seemed to Frances the lengthy welcome was more than a little overdone, more interested in making the Cromwells' stay as much beneficial to themselves as to the Cromwells. It took ages before they were allowed to board the coaches.

The house they were to stay in was close to St Bride's Church in the finer part of town. One of the very few fine buildings, it had tall rectangular windows, neat, well-kept gardens and an impressive drive. Every room was high and spacious, including the two for Frances and Mary.

'A room each!' Frankie's eyes were round as saucers and so were Mary's. They had never known such luxury. Coming up in the world was wonderful. 'And such a large bed! And all mine.'

'And mine too,' echoed Mary, rushing back into her own room.

Lettie did her best to divide her time between the two, unpacking for both of them while they raced in and out of each other's room, trying chairs and stools – Frankie's upholstered in green brocade and Mary's in blue – fingering the matching drapes at the windows, peeping into clothes chests, and leaping on and off each other's beds, both of which had carved posts to the ceiling with brocade curtains and hangings, vigorously testing their softness to the consternation of poor Lettie trying to unpack.

'Oh, miss!' she complained as neatly piled clothing toppled under the bouncing Frances was giving her bed, only to let out another protest as Mall came running in to throw herself on to the same bed, the pair of them with shrieks and squeals becoming half buried in strewn garments and the bed's voluminous luxury.

'Frankie! Mall!' Their mother's voice, quiet but firm as she appeared at the door, put a stop to the romps. 'The voyage has wearied me quite enough without all this noise from the both of you. I suspect Lettie has had enough of you also. If you cannot rest, kindly allow others to do so.'

Their mother departing to her own rooms, Lettie gave a giggle as they clambered off the bed.

Embarrassed at being scolded before the maid, Frances found herself snappy. 'What do you find so funny?' she demanded, but seeing the mess they had made, she immediately relented. 'I'm sorry, Lettie. Perhaps we can help you to put them away.'

'Of course not, miss.' The small round face, glum a moment earlier, broke into a smile. 'It's no trouble to me. And then I'll lay out your hairbrushes on one of them tables.'

Frances regarded the two elegant little tables of polished elmwood each standing before tall narrow windows through which the glow from a setting sun flooded in to gild the rich wood panelling and timber traceries of the ceiling. She pointed at one of the tables.

'That one, I think, Lettie.' Mary was leaning over the other, peering through the small square window panes.

'Frankie, you can see for miles. Come and see.'

Joining her, Frankie's hazel eyes widened. Beyond the low rooftops of the city, moist rich greens that only the damp airs of Ireland could produce spread out almost meeting the sky but for the low line of the distant Dublin Mountains, their rounded summits a purple haze.

'It's so much better than London. I think I shall like it here.'

'Like it!' Mary became suddenly animated. 'We'll do more than like it. We'll explore it – the whole city – meet lots of important people and there'll be banquets and parties. Look at all those who came to greet us. Do you realise how important we have become? Daughters of the Lord Lieutenant of Ireland. We shall be the centre of attention.'

Racing out, she returned with a dress the colour of ripe corn and held it against herself. 'I shall wear this at our very first reception. And you?'

Hurrying over, Frankie selected one from those now laid out tidily on her bed. It was of pale green watered silk, made for her especially to come here. Reverently picking it up, her thoughts flew instantly to Mr Jeremiah White. Surely such a dress couldn't but draw his eyes – that was if good fortune brought him to Papa's first reception – a vain hope but one that filled her with a rush of excited anticipation.

'This one,' she said purposefully. Mary pulled a face.

'We will clash. You in green and I in gold. We'll look like decorations on a reception platform.'

Frances frowned. 'They complement each other. You merely have to glance out there to see that.' Dropping the dress back on the bed, she all but dragged her sister over to the window. 'See? Green fields, and there's one full of ripe hay in the distance. God Himself shows us how well one complements the other.' She paused to gaze again at the view. 'You are right, Mall, it *is* a most beautiful land.'

And if Mr White were to remain in Papa's service, and if

he were to turn appreciative eyes in her direction, it would become even more beautiful.

Mary had cast her a sideways glance. 'Then do look as though you think so. Your face has gone quite long. You've been falling into a reverie for weeks now – like some lovelorn scullery maid.'

'Don't be silly!' cried Frances, turning away. But Mary's interruption to her thoughts had made her anxious. Was she far too young to have such feelings for a man? And were they that evident?

'I wish we were back home.'

Mary meant London. Dublin was proving not the grand city she had imagined. London had its fair share of squalor, as did any city, but it had its fine buildings too – the banqueting hall at Whitehall, Westminster Cathedral, St Paul's, and many fine churches. Dublin was unrelieved squalor – the decaying centre of a decomposing body. Few of its shabby buildings had been replaced since the time of Henry VIII. Its churches were dilapidated, its cathedral ruinous, the city walls with their eight once proud gates and nine towers in a poor state of repair. What had struck romantic on that first winding route to their new home through streets even narrower than London's Shambles had by September become wearisome by their unrelieved poverty – all except the few fine houses where the Cromwells resided. Added to that, the weather.

'I've never known so much rain,' sighed Mary after a continuous fortnight of it. 'Remember how warm and sunny it was when we arrived? Now one cannot venture out except by carriage, the streets are so awash with mud and night soil. We have to wear our pattens wherever we go to keep our feet out of the mud.'

Frances glanced up from the supper table with disgust towards the window where their Irish serving maid,

Amelia, was on the point of drawing the curtains. September clouds threatening yet more rain, six o'clock and already Amelia was having to light candles.

'I too wish we were in London. It's becoming so boring here.'

Bridget, who had been supervising Jane's nurse in sitting her up at the table, turned her eyes sharply upon Frances.

'This is your home now. Why can't you be content?'

'I would be,' Frances shot at her, 'if Papa were here. No matter where we go it seems he must always be absent.' Without Papa what chance was there of her and Mr White ever meeting?

Bridget's expression had grown affronted. 'Do you not think I too feel that absence, that I long to have my husband here beside me? But he, like Papa, has his duties, so I pray the Lord gives me the fortitude to endure his absence. If you have so little to do as to be bored, you'd do well to spend a little more time in prayer for patience, which you both seem to lack . . .'

'I pray well enough,' Frances flared back at her, 'for *all* blessings.'

'Most of them selfish, I've no doubt.'

'Yours too are as selfish – thinking of your husband and no one else.'

'My dears, please!' As Bridget's face became thunderous, their mother held up a conciliatory hand. 'Let us just be thankful for what we already have and pray earnestly for the safe return of our dear men. Now then . . .'

Clasping her hands together, she bent her head. Around the table her daughters obediently followed suit.

Prayers over, she turned her eyes towards her youngest daughter as Amelia brought in Scotch collops, brawn, pease pottage, bread, with ginger cake to follow.

'I'm concerned by your discontent, Frankie. We have frequent enough callers. We take up all invitations. And surely you and Mall are pleased with the young men who clamour to be introduced.'

'We are, Mama,' Mary broke in, but a look from Frances, who was always complaining how dull the young men were at their social gatherings, stopped her.

'They're either doleful Puritans or callow, fawning Anglo-Irish rustics,' Frances grumbled.

But she couldn't help feeling for Mary, her own mind going over some of the people they'd met so far, all of them gushing over the Cromwell women, and so boring: the wife of Colonel Jones, who'd gallantly broken out of Ormonde and Inchiquin's siege of Dublin last May and hadn't stopped talking about it as related to her by her husband; Lady Broghill, whose husband once had Royalist sympathies but whom Papa had won over; and Viscountess Ranelagh, so staunchly Puritan that she reminded Frances of a stiff petticoat. There was Catherine Boyle, the simpering sister of Broghill, and there was Colonel George Monck's prim wife – all of them stiff-necked and their sons exactly the same. To put it mildly, she wouldn't give a fig for any one of them.

Amelia came into the room to hand Mama a letter. 'A messenger has come wi' this, ma'am,' she enlightened in her slow Irish brogue. 'Oi t'ink it moit be from yur hosband.'

Everyone became instantly attentive as Elizabeth took it and swiftly broke the seal, unfolding the paper. Her face broke into a smile. 'Your father has taken Drogheda,' she said.

'And he'll be coming home?' asked Frances eagerly. Surely Mr White would be with him. At last they'd meet, she was sure of it now.

'We pray he will,' returned her mother.

Protected though it was by stout walls and the River

Boyne, Drogheda had not dismayed Oliver. His menacing artillery drawn up from the south, all day deserters from Lord Inchiquin's army had trickled out to join the Parliamentarians, and despite the defenders on the walls, the whole town lay silent as though already defeated.

'This will be an easy victory,' he predicted to his comptroller. 'Our men are in good spirits. That priest-ridden populace knows not which way to turn.'

The town might remain silently brooding. Outside its walls those in their hovels showed no fear of the invading army. Bold as robins they had come into camp – mostly barefoot women in linen head-shawls, a crucifix dangling quite unashamedly between their breasts as they sold food to the soldiers.

'They are to be well paid for their services,' Cromwell ordered. 'There must be no cause for complaints of plunder.'

They were orders wisely obeyed after witnessing two soldiers hanged for stealing some hens on the way here. Cromwell knew his men and they knew him. Under his command they were an army to be reckoned with and they were proud of that.

He had issued his demand for Sir Arthur Aston, commander of Drogheda whom Ormonde had deputised, to surrender the town and avoid bloodshed. 'If this is refused,' he'd warned, 'you will have no cause to blame me.'

'He dare not refuse,' he said when his comptroller ventured to speculate on that possibility, 'when his own men are coming over to our side. The country people are trading with our lads, happy to see us as pigeons in a field of corn. Have no fear, my dear Captain Tomlins, today the Lord of Hosts is with us, and Drogheda will open its gates to us in fear at our strength in the Lord.'

And hardly had he settled down to wait, Aston's reply was brought to his tent. Full of confidence, Oliver broke the seal, but as he scanned the contents, his face grew crimson. Crumpling the terse communiqué between blunt fingers, he tossed it from him.

'By the living God!' he burst out. 'What's the man thinking? He knows our strength. He knows well the rules of siege.'

Confidence in easy victory dissolving into hot rage, he leapt up, overturning his stool, and stomped about the tent, pushing aside any who got in his way.

'Does the man not realise that spurning invitation to surrender under siege places in peril all those under his protection – soldier and civilian alike? Every townsman and townswoman must be regarded a combatant and if needs be, slaughtered as such. *He* has decreed this, not I. If he wishes an infusion of blood, so be it. With God's help we will storm that accursed town!'

Fury unabated, he issued commands, his officers frantically relaying them to their companies, and all through the next day of his great siege guns and field pieces mercilessly hammered the southern defences without stop.

Men cheered as St Mary's Church, built solidly into the south-west corner of Drogheda's stout walls, was reduced to rubble. But those walls were six feet thick at the base and twenty feet high. A day of pounding made many breaches but only wide enough for foot soldiers to enter. Dusk found Cromwell sitting on his horse watching the bombardment with growing impatience, his ears ringing from the terrific gunfire that made every man's shout seem as though he were whispering. In the pit of Oliver's stomach was a grinding pain that often occurred when his temper got the better of him.

'We are pressed for time,' he finally bellowed at the comptroller of the artillery. 'Cease bombardment and send in the foot.'

The man was startled. 'Sir, without the horse they'll be

beaten back.' But his superior had reached a high heat of practically uncontrollable passion. 'No time for the breaches to be widened more. Send in the foot!' he roared, so demented that the officer quickly bowed his head and ran off to carry out orders.

It was soon obvious the men would never get into the town without the support of the horse as around narrow, rubble-strewn gaps a confusion of bodies became locked in terrible combat, the defenders far more reckless than he had given them credit for.

A trooper came galloping up to him, reining his horse cruelly to a halt. 'We make no headway, sir!' he shouted, hardly able to get his breath. 'The horse can get in only singly. Many of our officers are dead. Sir, we can make no headway!'

'Can you not indeed?' The crack of Cromwell's voice made the man's horse wheel and dance, eyes rolling, spume flying from its reddened muzzle, while Cromwell's own mount started back in alarm. Blood pounded in his temples. 'I'll show you how to make headway, sir,' he shrieked, 'or die in the attempt. Summon the cavalry to follow me!'

He was off, hardly had orders been given, racing for the town at full gallop like one demented, his cavalry streaming after him; in their wake followed foot soldiers enthused by their leader's example, their blood up, their battle cries travelling ahead of them across the damp green fields.

The cost was terrible, but Cromwell was with them. And now there was reinforcement under Captain Ewers. The press forcing men and horses through the gaps in the walls like a flood, the stout defenders of Drogheda could only fall back as eight thousand troops poured over them into the town like hounds at the kill. Seeing only an enemy that had defied them, the soldiers went after anything that moved – shooting, stabbing, dashing little heads against walls, burning every house and church together with those who cowered, terrified, inside. Women, children, it made no difference to the blood-crazed. Cromwell himself was powerless to stem the frenzy that had come upon his men, they themselves consumed by his very own rage.

News of Drogheda's massacre spread quickly. Small towns such as Dunkalk and Trim surrendered readily to avoid repetition. It was as well, thought Oliver. There had been blood enough, inevitable in battle, but needlessly spilled at Drogheda.

Try as he might to lay blame for the carnage at Drogheda at the feet of the foolhardy Sir Arthur Aston, his own part in it pricked at Cromwell like small needles for having lost his temper in that way. Nothing ever upset Oliver more than the realisation of having fallen victim to his own rages, and he was ashamed.

Dublin didn't see it that way, nor did England. To them he was a mighty hero who had caused the north of Ireland to quake, and so with small losses on both sides from then onward, commanders such as Colonel Venables and Sir Charles Coote were easily able to subdue most of the northern towns and secure the whole area without too much bloodshed.

With only the south remaining, all Ireland would soon be subdued. Cromwell, the man for the job, entered Dublin to flying banners and cheers of welcome. Smiling, waving to the excited crowds, he graciously accepted the praise showered upon him. But to himself he made a vow never to allow the heat of passion as he had experienced at Drogheda to overcome him ever again.

'I've never seen Papa so merry.'

The family were at the banquet given in Cromwell's honour by Lord and Lady Broghill, who had lately become friends with him. Seated opposite her father but a few places down from him at the long table, Frances had hardly taken her eyes off him. His brightness did her good, but Mary huffed and wrinkled her nose.

'I'd rather he wouldn't voice his merriness so loudly,' she said. 'He hasn't ceased singing at the top of his lungs since returning home. It's not as though he has a pleasing voice. I've never heard anything so tuneless, and that's a pity for one who loves music as he does.'

Oliver enjoyed nothing better than listening to music, and especially to one or the other of his daughters playing the spinet.

'Well, I'm glad he's happy,' Frances retaliated as her empty plate was taken up by one of the waiting staff.

Mary huffed again. 'It seems to me he overdoes his happiness. Almost as though he doesn't feel as happy as he would have us think.'

Wandering among the after-dinner guests, what Mary had said made Frances thoughtful. Perhaps Mall was right, he was being just a little too happy to be true, his rasping laughter emanating back to her through the clusters of people.

Even so, she couldn't help smiling at the reactions his singing could produce at home. At the first preliminary clearing of his throat, an amused smile would appear on every face from their cook Mrs O'Lerhily to Mama. All except Bridget, who hadn't forgiven him for making Colonel James, a hero of Dublin, Second in Command instead of her husband, who was still pacifying Papist rebels in the south.

Now, to Lady Broghill's confusion, he had requested music, which very few Puritans would dream of allowing. He had even danced a little jig, to the amusement of his host, urging everyone to join him. Soon the natural exuberance of Irish blood – only partly submerged beneath its Anglo surface – came pouring out until, with her head spinning from so much whooping and squealing, Frances hurried away to a quieter place to think about all this mad blood that seemed to have got into her father.

Every room in the Broghill home was full of guests with questions and admiration for the Lord Lieutenant's youngest daughter. She should have been flattered but it only heightened her need for seclusion.

Finally she found a deserted long gallery at the top of the house with tall windows along one side. The now faint sounds of revelry from below made the gallery even more hushed and she took delight in the luxury of being completely alone, praying no one would come to disturb this sweet stillness. She gazed down at the fine Broghill estates. The night sky – clear for once – allowed a bright and frosty three-quarter moon to throw the half denuded clumps of trees into relief, their dry old leaves fluttering to earth like silvery snowflakes.

A soft footfall on the polished wood floor at the far end of the gallery made her turn sharply, prepared to smile at the owner of the feet. Seconds later her heart leapt with joy.

'Mr White!'

Instead of the clerical suit, he was in a buff uniform, cutting the most gallant figure she had ever seen. Standing quite still, her heart seemed to be all but overpowering her at the easy gait with which he strode towards her. She noted too how wind-tanned his lean cheeks were as he halted just the width of a hand's shake from her.

'Lady Frances . . .' His tone was formal. 'Have I disturbed you?'

'N-not at all,' she found herself stammering ineptly, and no wonder. She had become so breathless it was a miracle she could speak at all.

'I wasn't certain that you'd remember me,' he said, his voice low. It sounded quite seductive though she was sure he hadn't meant it to be.

With difficulty she recovered enough composure to become aware that she had grown taller since last they'd met, no longer having to look up at him. Somewhat idiotically the knowledge sent a bound of joy through her.

'Indeed I remember, sir.' It was hard to compose herself. To appear even more composed, she brought her hands to the front, lightly holding the fingers of one hand in the other, the way that a matronly woman would. But all the time she felt far from controlled.

'I am very glad you remember,' he was saying. It sounded flippant but the dark narrow eyes were holding hers in their steady gaze, seemingly full of deeper meaning that made her cheeks grow warm and she dropped her gaze to avoid the scrutiny.

'I did not see you among the returning troops,' she said quickly.

'Did you not?' There was amusement in his voice. 'Then I take it you assumed I wasn't among them.'

'Were you then?' she countered sharply.

'I was not.' Her face tightening angrily, he hurried on but far less playfully. 'I didn't arrive until this evening. I've since been looking for you. Lady Frances . . .' He seemed to bend towards her. 'My wish was to see you the first moment I could. But certain duties frustrated any earlier arrival. Lady Fran . . . Frances . . .'

He reached out and took one of her hands. When she made no effort to pull away, his grip firmed, his hands cool on hers sending a small shiver of delight through her. Protocol cried out that she should hold herself rigid, and that not to was unseemly. But the sound of his voice was flowing over her like honey.

'Frances,' he repeated. 'Throughout this entire expedition I've been able to think of little else but you. I hoped that in return your thoughts, here in Dublin, were of little else but me. Dare I hope it was so?'

Allowing herself no time to reflect on what she was doing, Frances inclined her head, felt his fingers tighten correspondingly on her to gently draw her closer to him.

'Am I being too bold?' his voice came in a whisper.

'You are indeed, Mr White,' she returned, but her own whisper contradicted those words.

He was so near now, his face so close to hers that she could feel the warmth of his breath, such a sweet warmth, yet his words were hardly audible.

'Dare I be bolder, ask that you give thought to using the name I would most dearly wish to hear on your lips – Jeremiah? No, not even that, but Jerry.'

For a moment she remained silent. Her heart was beating with a strange and heavy sickening thud in the knowledge of what she was doing, allowing herself to become familiar with him, and they alone in this gallery. She was sure he too could feel its thumping.

She should have left then, hurried away to the safety of other people, safe from him, and herself. Instead, she looked up into his face to find his lips on level with hers. Before she could move back; his face had tilted towards hers so that his lips brushed hers in the briefest, lightest kiss. Like his hands, his lips were cold, yet the touch of them sent a sensation through every inch of her. In his buff uniform he was her soldier, her dream soldier. Before her startled gaze she saw him step back.

'Forgive me,' he said quietly. 'I've been too presumptuous.'

'No!' The word burst from her. 'Jeremiah . . . Jerry . . .'

A movement at the far end of the gallery caught her. Instantly filled with alarm, Frances turned. There stood Lord Lieutenant Cromwell, gazing steadily at them. How long he had been there, she had no idea, but panic and guilt shot through her.

As Jerry, hearing her gasp, turned to look in the direction

of her stare, the stern, thick-set figure signalled to him. The tuneless, nasal voice, although not raised, carried with menacing clarity the entire length of the gallery.

'A moment from your diversions, if you please, Mr White.'

Five

1650

During the few days Oliver remained in Dublin before leaving for the south there was plenty of time for hawking and hunting.

'Excellent game!' he called to Lady Broghill as the ladies rode out to watch and applaud. 'Seldom have I seen such grouse and pheasant, and woodcock too. As for hares, they are as abundant as rats. You've a fine, well stocked-country, dear madam, and indeed you yourself do the hunting justice.'

Riding with the men, as skilled with a fowling-piece as any of them and bringing down a deer on the second day, she graciously acknowledged his applause. 'Tomorrow we might go after boar.'

'Boar, eh?'

'We have wolves here too,' she added with pride.

'Those we must see,' he announced as they rode stirrup to stirrup, she as straight in the saddle as any man despite riding side-saddle as women usually did, though mostly it was Oliver who led the field, agile as a man half his age. Having brought down a fine stag he threw himself from his horse to wait for the others to catch up. When they finally did, he put his arms about his two youngest daughters to lead them to view his success.

'Come and inspect the kill, my little wenches,' he bellowed happily and laughed loudly as Mary squealed at the sight of a bleeding, fallen animal. Without resorting to the anticipated squeals Frances acknowledged her father's skills dutifully but soberly, his warmth towards her as large as ever.

He'd laid no blame at her door for the incident with herself and Mr White. Even so, Jeremiah White had made his departure the very next day on some errand for Papa, and although she dared not ask what the errand was, she'd been made quite aware that Papa had no intention of her and his young chaplain continuing their budding relationship.

If he had any idea of the strange raw emptiness his move had left inside her, Papa gave no indication of it as he teased her, encouraging her to join in the merriment of those few days before he was due to leave. She continued to smile charmingly at his guests but her heartache she kept to herself.

It was November before she finally felt able to tell someone about it.

'But please,' she begged Mary as they sat side by side on the bed in the seclusion of Mary's room, 'don't tell a soul what I've told you. Swear.'

'I swear,' Mary said lightly, more interested in the romance of it all, her dark eyes forming large orbs as she regarded her sister. 'How can you be sure you really love him after such a short time?'

'How can I be sure?' echoed Frances, staring abjectly towards the window. As usual it was raining. Soft Irish rain, gentle but persistent, like its people. 'I know how much I long to see him again. When he kissed me, so lightly, I did not protest.'

'Ah,' responded Mary sagaciously.

But Frances needed to be honest. 'There was no time to protest. Papa saw us. He was standing there watching us, so quietly, and we were taken aback. We never even saw him arrive.'

'Had he not been there,' persisted Mary, 'would you have allowed Mr White to kiss you a second time without your protesting?'

'I really don't know.'

'I'm sure you would have. I think you love him.'

'If only I knew what love really was,' sighed Frances.

Mary was silent for a while, wrapped in the romance of it all. 'If I felt such yearning as you say you have,' she murmured after a while, 'I would say I was in love.'

Frances slid off the bed and went to the dressing table. She took up Mary's hairbrush and began running it through her heavy ringlets, careless of the destruction. Finally she gave a decisive shrug.

'What does it matter? It's only to be expected that Papa is hoping for a fine and suitable marriage contract when I am of a proper age to wed. He is becoming a very prominent figure, bringing all the north of Ireland under Parliament rule.' She was making an effort at a brave little speech. 'It was wrong of me to have embarrassed him so, and I suppose Mr White did behave audaciously, approaching me as he did while I was alone. I cannot blame Papa for being displeased. After all . . .'

The brave effort died away. She couldn't blame Jeremiah White. She could have blamed herself, but all the time a niggling of accusation attached itself to Papa, the way he had crept up on them, had stood listening without so much as a discreet cough to alert them. How long had he been standing there? It had been most unfair of him. Frances stared unfocused through the rain-splattered window pane, the hairbrush idle in her hands.

As winter gave way to spring, Elizabeth Cromwell began to grow restless.

'Dorothy is nearing her time,' she stated fretfully. 'And she so far away from us.' For some reason it did not occur to her that Dorothy had her own parents almost on her doorstep and probably didn't need her at all. But it was an excuse. 'Poor Richard away from us all. And poor Doll, her first child, I should be with her for the birth. I really do not know what keeps me in this dismal country when I am needed far more urgently elsewhere.'

Frances didn't know what kept them there either, with her father busy bringing southern Ireland into subjection with the help of her brother Henry and Bridget's husband Ireton. The plan had been for the whole family to follow and winter in Wexford. But the weather had been appalling and Wexford had been taken only after much bloodshed and ruination, hardly a place for the women to use as their winter quarters. Added to this, the pieces of furniture Mama had insisted on taking with her to make her stay more comfortable were raided by brigands in the Wicklow Mountains with such cheek as only the Irish could possess. Elizabeth was utterly distraught.

'They are heathens, all of them!' she wept when she heard the news. 'It's said that when the Devil showed our Saviour all the kingdoms of the earth he would not show Him Ireland, reserving it for himself. That I can quite believe!'

Obliged to return to Dublin, it needed only that last straw for her to see her daughter-in-law's coming confinement as an excuse to leave Ireland altogether. 'Besides,' she said determinedly, 'it's best to make the crossing before the March gales make it impossible.'

All winter Oliver had been sick from ague that plagued the Irish bogs. But now his health had improved. 'So there's little to keep me here,' she wrote to him and he agreed it best she did return to England.

Bridget was to remain. 'My place is beside my husband,' she told her mother primly. So Elizabeth took only Mary and Frances back to England with her, to the delight of

Frances, certain that this was where her father had probably kept his young chaplain, out of harm's way.

'It's so good to be back home.' Leaning from the parlour window of Dick's charming Hampshire house, Frances took in a deep breath of the crisp morning air.

A rivalry of twittering robins were claiming territory and the echoing trill of blackbirds coming into song brought a wonderful sense of the familiar. Even the raucous chatter of magpies was a joy to hear. There were no magpies in Ireland.

It had been so pleasing, disembarking to encounter the plain-spoken, wooden-faced Welsh innkeeper after the ingratiating servility of Irish smiles that never quite reached the eyes on speaking to Englishmen. Ireland had possessed a totally different culture, but Frances did not quite realise how different until returning here. Wales had its mountains as did Ireland, Wiltshire its lonely vistas and Hampshire lush green fields and woodlands. Ireland had all these things, in fact a green far more vivid, but there had been a wildness that even the loneliest mountaintop in England couldn't rival. It was good to be back with familiar sights and sounds and people.

'Frankie.' Her mother's voice startled her. 'Close the window please.'

She glanced over her shoulder. 'It's open a little way.'

'Nevertheless, we do not want Doll taking a chill with the baby ready to be born.'

'Will it be today?' Mary looked up excitedly from the book she'd been reading.

'She has had some mild pains,' said her mother. 'But only the good Lord can say when it will be born. The first is never quick, but please God it will be easy for her. Frankie, do close the window.'

Dorothy's confinement in an upper chamber, the offending

window could hardly affect her. Frances did as she was told, but a little petulantly.

She was bored.

'May we take a little walk then? It's such a clement morning. Mary and I could walk into the village.'

Mary was on her feet immediately. 'Dick did say we could buy some comfits. He has an account with the shopkeeper there.'

Her mother smiled. 'Your brother isn't made of money, though he imagines he is. Very well, put on warm cloaks. March isn't a month to be trusted.'

It was fun gazing at the village houses, buying the sweet pastry from the little bakery there, wandering back, on their way examining the tight little buds of windflowers and primroses, giggling over virtually nothing. Reaching home, they were met by Dick's housekeeper in plain dress and apron who ushered them through the house to a small room at the rear.

'Bide here awhile, my ladies,' she fussed. 'Keep out of the way, and pray for the child's safe and swift delivery.'

'Is the baby to be born?' Frances blurted, amazed by the swiftness of events in their absence.

'It is. But first-born do take an inordinate time to get into this world. We can only trust—'

From the top of the house came a woman's cry, drawn out and high-pitched. The housekeeper glanced upwards.

'Lord bless us! I must be upstairs lest I'm needed. Now stay here, my ladies. And don't go prying and peeking. If you're hungry, Mrs Harris will give you something from the kitchen.'

Another drawn-out pathetic cry sent her scurrying off, leaving the two girls to listen for the rest of the day to urgent footsteps about the house and the desperate fight Dorothy was having.

Richard came in from the fields once to see how things

were, then, as white as a sheet, quickly departed. Mrs Harris, the cook, gave them some stew with neat's tongue and a tansy pudding to follow, but it was hard to arouse any appetite for what was continuing in the upper room.

Darkness gathering, their mother came to say they were to sleep in a room on the ground floor. Truckle-beds were put up for them, their own room being too close to that where Doll was in labour.

'Please God it will only be for the one night,' Mama said significantly, her soft round face pale and drawn as though she had felt every shred of the girl's pain. 'She is strong and healthy but should it go on too long . . .'

She left the rest unsaid. It was plain that a woman could stand only so much before her strength gave out, no matter how healthy she was.

Sleep was impossible, the night rent by intermittent cries, dying away to be renewed, shrill and piercing. Sometime during the evening Richard made another brief appearance, his soft brown eyes full of distress for his wife as he made yet another hasty exit, saying he had to see to some beasts in his barns, refusing the supper Mrs Harris had earlier laid out waiting for him.

In their temporary sleeping chamber, Frances and Mary lay in their narrow beds staring up at the low ceiling. Frances felt her bedcover damp from her own perspiration as the hours crawled by. Then just before dawn the screams suddenly renewed in strength. They seemed to tear through her flesh. Then as suddenly they ceased. Frances sat bolt upright, listening. Seconds of silence pounded in her ears. Mary had also shot upright.

'Oh, Frankie. She's dead.'

It was a task to stem her rising panic. Then came a thin high sound, uncertain and wavering but swiftly gathering strength.

Mary leapt off her bed. 'The baby! It's born! It's alive!'

She stopped abruptly then went on with fear in her tone. 'But what of Doll?'

Barefooted, in their nightgowns, they raced from the room, down the passage and into the hall in time to see their mother descending the stairs. She smiled wearily at them.

'I must find Richard.'

'He said he would be in the barns,' Frances supplied. 'Is Doll . . . ?'

Her mother's face conveyed nothing but fatigue of the last seventeen hours. She made to speak, but the main door bursting open stopped her. Richard, with one arm holding the door back as though it might close on him again and leave him outside, looked as though he hadn't slept, or if he had, had done so in his clothes, his hair hanging dull and uncombed, his russet coat creased, its linen collar usually white and immaculate, far from crisp.

'I heard the child cry.' His voice was the shout of a man caught by fear and confusion in a woman's domain. 'It's born then?'

His mother went towards him. 'You have a daughter,' she said, but it seemed to mean nothing to him.

'And Doll . . . does she survive?'

Elizabeth smiled through her fatigue. 'She survives very well, Dick. Worn out by her exertions, undoubtedly. A longish labour and the child was large even for a girl. But Doll did very well. You have a fine brave wife, Dick, and a healthy, comely daughter.'

'Thanks be to God!' The prayer came like a sigh as he sank to his knees exactly where he had stood, his fingers entwined, his head bent – a simple gesture which the women immediately adopted, followed by the two servants who were present in the hall, all six in silent gratitude for the safe deliverance of a loved one and her child while the chill morning crept in through the still open door.

* * *

Dorothy named her baby Elizabeth Ann after her husband's mother and her own.

'For all your loving help,' she told them both. 'Without which I am certain I would have succumbed.'

Although her own mother had been there, it was to the quiet and competent Elizabeth she owed the most thanks, and Ann Mayor was content to concur with that, not knowing what she would have done without the other woman's calming presence. Doll had named her daughter Elizabeth, but was soon cooing the shorter name Beth with her grandmothers incessantly hovering over her as well as getting on splendidly with each other.

But restlessness began to overtake Elizabeth Cromwell. 'Parliament is calling for my husband's return,' she told her daughter-in-law's mother. 'I have to be in London to welcome him.'

For Ann this was a blow. Given to woolly-headedness, she had come much to rely on her capable guest. 'Is there not still plenty for him to do in Ireland?'

'He has competent commanders in Henry Ireton and my son Henry,' she was told proudly, leaving no argument.

Doll too was sad. 'I shall miss you sorely,' she lamented, the baby at her breast as she sat in bed to regain her strength. Beth was a greedy baby, keeping her mother stick thin so that Dorothy's blue eyes looked large in her wistful face.

'You've your loving family about you,' Elizabeth consoled her. 'And your husband is with you.'

Dorothy's mood lifted a little. 'Will you be writing to your husband to tell him of the birth of his son's child?'

'He would be more consoled,' said her mother-in-law, suddenly stern, 'to read it from your own hand. There are times he has been deeply grieved that you often fail to write to him. I believe at one time he had to ask your father to prompt you.'

It was a mild rebuke but Doll's eyes filled with tears and she cuddled little Beth closer to her. 'I did write to him,' she said tremulously.

'For which, at the time, he was considerably heartened.' It was not easy to keep the stiffness from her reply. She understood the girl's natural depression after giving birth making her want to do little more than lie abed and enjoy her own tiny world with her new baby. But Oliver had been very hurt by her earlier silences, he himself in a fit of depression after being laid low by fever from the strange airs of Ireland, calling her a promise-breaker.

'He did not expect to hear often from Dick,' Elizabeth continued resolutely, 'knowing Dick's idleness in such things. But he hoped that you, as his wife, would have tried to guide him in his filial duty to his father and also may I add in his pursuit of the Lord in which he also appears to have failed. But my husband's greatest sorrow was that you yourself did not write to him of your own free will until reminded by him through your father. But let us not dwell on past grievances.'

She came and patted Dorothy's hand. 'Dick's father will be consoled well enough to hear from your own hand that he's now grandfather to Dick's child.'

On Oliver's return in May, leading Members of Parliament and Council of State at Windsor Castle put on a great formal welcome for their hero. Many members of his family were there too. Among them were Betty and her husband, who had managed to make the journey with their two young sons. So were Dick and Dorothy, a wet-nurse attending little Beth. And of course Frances and Mary. The only members of the immediate family absent were Bridget and Henry Ireton and Oliver's eldest son Henry, all still in Ireland.

The old staterooms of Windsor were crowded. Eminent

people in fine clothes jostled each other as they waited for the Lord Lieutenant of Ireland. Most of the furnishings were allowed to remain after the despatch of their royal owner, and made a splendid setting. Yet Frances couldn't feel at ease here. It was as if the dead King's ghost still hovered about the place, inviting some future ill on the man who appeared to be rapidly taking his place.

It was 1650 – a whole year since the King's death, time enough to have put such childish imaginings behind her. Since meeting the handsome Mr White, Frances felt she had indeed grown up. She hadn't laid eyes on him these past eight months yet still his lean, gentle face haunted her almost as much as the imagined ghost of the dead King, the one making her shiver with delight, the other in horror.

'I've no liking for this place,' she whispered to her mother as they waited with the rest. Her mother gave her a tolerant smile.

'It is a little crowded I admit. But your father has proved himself a great man. People are bound to flock to see him.'

'It isn't that,' Frances began, but a great stir beginning to ripple through the waiting crowd put an end to what she might have said.

The great doors being heaved open, in strode the purposeful, heavy-set figure of her father. Despite the greatness of the occasion and his new standing with the Commonwealth he was as carelessly dressed as ever. Dear Papa. He would never change. Frances felt a wave of pride flow over her as she beheld him. In that instant her father's presence dashed away the cold ghost she had felt hovering among the rafters of the state room as the walls echoed to a huge burst of applause.

Lengthy speeches done, the banquet over, all the after-dinner discussions concluded, Oliver was finally allowed to retreat with his family to the apartments that had been set aside for them.

In the comfort of a sumptuously furnished withdrawing room he lounged in a large, heavy chair before the fire in the huge grate lit against a slightly chilly night. The rosy light of the fire and of the rushlights in their portable stands flickered upon the faces of his loved ones.

'I've long looked forward to an evening like this,' he sighed contentedly.

His long-stemmed pipe sending up a wreath of aromatic blue smoke, a pot of mulled ale at his elbow, his collar and jacket loosened, he sat with one leg crooked over the other. Savouring the precious moment, he gazed at the pleasant homely face of his wife, her eyes gentle, her mouth composed – a loyal loving wife, quiet-natured yet with an inner strength that made him ever proud of her.

There were his two pretty youngest daughters, their eyes dancing, their lips expressive. Mary, the quieter of the two, was ambitious like himself, but patiently waiting out her childhood. In two years, perhaps sooner, he'd begin looking for a suitable husband for her, or at least presentable suitors for her to choose from.

Frances was more of a problem – though he loved her dearly – her heart forever leading her head. Always so wilful yet sometimes she appeared the older of the two, so tall she was, with such an adult look about her.

Then there was Doll – fair as an angel but still thin from her confinement. And Richard. What of Richard? Handsome but weak. Idle. Content to drift on a sea of fine living. A disappointment. But loved for all that.

There was John Claypole, Betty's husband. Gentle-mannered, round-faced, passive-lipped, a man too gentle to hold any military office, a designer of buildings, an architect, and to Betty a desirable and loving husband.

Oliver's eyes roved towards his favourite daughter, her two sons – who should have been in bed – playing at her feet with draught counters. Of all his daughters, Betty was the prettiest, the most sweet-natured and high-spirited, a defender of the fallen. Oliver's grey eyes grew pensive. If only her health matched her liveliness.

'So long since I've sat with my family about me,' he mused aloud.

Sitting by his knee, Frances, absorbed in playing cat's cradle with a length of coloured thread, glanced up at him, almost challengingly.

'You'll not be going away again, Papa?'

He reached down to fondle the brown curls. 'My earnest prayer is not to. Scotland continues to proclaim young Charles Stuart their king, Presbyterian though they are. He, the cunning man, has sworn to uphold their Covenant. It could cause war between our two countries and me to leave my loving family yet again.' An angry glint touched his eyes. 'God curse that young upstart! The Papist front door now closed to him in Ireland, he rattles the locks of the Presbyterian back door, beguiling the Scots. He would even bring conflict between Englishmen and our Scottish brothers to gain his throne.' Pausing, he saw consternation on every face and quickly relaxed back into his chair. 'But there, we have an able Commander-in-Chief in Thomas Fairfax. He will take our Army to Scotland if need arises. I have given fully of myself in Ireland. I shall not travel abroad again. The sea did not serve me well, and I am becoming too old for warring.'

'You're not old, Papa!' exclaimed Mary.

He laughed gruffly. 'Past my middle years, little one. I will hang up my laurels and regain my seat in Parliament instead.'

'A relief to us all,' remarked Elizabeth, turning her attention to the two boys, who had begun to squabble over the amount of draught pieces each had. 'It's time these two were abed, Betty.'

Betty, leaning forward to divide the draughts equally, sprang to their defence. 'It's such a special occasion today. Let them remain here a little longer. See, they're not tired.' Both children were staring wide-eyed and pleading at their elders and it was their grandfather who came to their aid.

'Let them remain. It's a joy to see young innocents at play after having witnessed so many fall dead of their wounds, be they Papist or—'

'Oh, Papa! I beg you!' Betty's face was anguished, and he hastily held up an apologetic hand towards her.

'Forgive me a soldier's insensitiveness. You the most tender-hearted of creatures, and here am I intruding upon that tenderness.' He let his hand fall on to the arm of his chair. 'Well, no more disharmony tonight. We shall enjoy each other's company. Let the children play till they fall asleep on the floor, then John and I will carry them to bed.' Sighing contentment, he took up his pipe. 'This is how I shall live out the rest of my days,' he murmured. 'Let the good Fairfax do the fighting, and God bless him.'

'Amen,' murmured John Claypole, who had remained quiet all this time. He was hastily echoed by Richard, bothering to look up from a book he was reading on farming, his thoughts far from this assembly.

'This is my place,' Oliver went on.

'And well deserved,' said John.

'By the way.' Oliver grew alert again. 'I've news. When we return to London it will not be to the house in King Street but to a finer one. Nearby Whitehall Palace. It is called the Cockpit, for such a place once stood there.'

His words immediately provoked excitement from Frances and Mary, but Elizabeth merely bit her lip, which he failed to notice, being so flattered and overcome by the noisy enthusiasm of his youngest daughters, whose questions he was readily answering.

'God bless Fairfax,' he repeated happily, seeing all his burdens lifted.

Six

1651

A fortnight later different words were spilling from his lips. 'Fairfax is beyond all belief!' he bellowed at Elizabeth in the privacy of their bedchamber of his new home.

From the large canopied bed, she watched him pace the room, any chance of her regaining sleep ruined. 'What has the man done?'

She had been enjoying such a good sleep, but Oliver had come bursting into their quarters as dawn was breaking, shouting to the servants who'd waited up for him to go back to bed. Stamping upstairs he'd flung open the bedroom door, closing it so violently that she'd awoken with a start.

Now she lay listening to his grunting, to his stomping about the room thumping one clenched fist against his leg. She was used to his rages. Like boiling pottage they bubbled and spat, doing little harm as far as she could see, and once taken off the fire, the heat would die away. It was his cold, silent anger that was disquieting, so in this instance she was not particularly put out – apart from being woken up so abruptly.

'Fairfax!' He spat out the name to her question. 'He has decided he has a conscience. Colonel Hutchinson and I have laboured this whole night with him on the matter.'

'On what matter?'

Oliver stopped pacing to glare at her. 'He says he will not lead any expedition of an offensive nature into Scotland. He insists it would be an obstacle to justice. Obstacle to justice!' He began pacing again. 'More like the man's lost his backbone. He thinks by this he can avoid war.'

'Can he?' Elizabeth sat up, resigned to no more sleep. Wearily she took the kerchief from her head and folded it neatly.

'He can not!' stormed Oliver, thumping one of the bedposts so hard that the whole bed shook. 'And I told him such. Said I to Fairfax, "That there will be war between us and Scotland is unavoidable." Hutchinson will bear out my words. I appealed to Fairfax, "Your Excellency will soon determine whether it be better to have this war in the bowels of another country or of our own, for it will be in one of them." Can you speculate what reply he gave to that?' Not waiting for her to answer, he raised his voice even louder. 'His reply, Elizabeth, was that human probabilities aren't sufficient ground to make war upon a neighbouring nation. Nothing I nor Hutchinson said would alter the man's mind. So with much heart-searching it will now be I who goes to Scotland.'

His anger spent, he sank down on a stool by the wall, hands clasped between his knees in an attitude of defeat. But it was those last words that brought Elizabeth hurrying to kneel consolingly before him.

'Oliver, my dearest, there are other generals, capable men. Some other rather than you could go in the place of Fairfax.'

His sigh went right through her. 'Who can I trust to lead an army into Scotland but myself? If Fairfax has faltered now, how many others will do so later?'

Wearily he got up and went to stand by the bed, one hand gripped into a fist against his temples while she watched helplessly.

'Sir Thomas Fairfax!' she spat contemptuously. 'He has ever been a man plagued by conscience. As he was at the King's trial, do you remember? A gallant officer, well liked, but his attitude doesn't surprise me.'

For all her contempt, she had felt some sympathy for the man, ruled as he was by his wife, Lady Ann, who had even gone to the King's trial to shout from the gallery that Oliver was a traitor, and had to be removed virtually at pistol point.

A lady had been seen around at that time wearing a mask, as some often did in public, making out to be a Cavalier activist, but those close to her knew it to be Lady Fairfax taking a high stand where her husband had been more circumspect in not being in accord with the King's execution.

His attitude, then as now, bewildered Elizabeth. One would have imagined him a more formidable leader – over six feet tall with hair and complexion so dark that he was popularly known as Black Tom, yet he was a man of fair mind and depth of thought. This morning, however, Elizabeth could feel no sympathy for him – it was because of him that her husband could be leaving his family and taking the English Army into Scotland.

She became aware of Oliver's bleak tone. 'I cannot risk a delay for conscience's sake until Charles Stuart comes leading a Scottish army into England. If I delay, it will be too late to halt him once he is over the border. He'll march on London unopposed. I must go to Scotland before that happens.'

That word 'I' made Elizabeth's heart sink. It was as though he was England and England was he, and as he had failed to sway Fairfax so she failed to sway Oliver.

By June twenty-sixth, Oliver was appointed General of the Forces of the Commonwealth with the title of Lord General, while the fortunate Fairfax melted quietly into retirement with his wife, for which Elizabeth felt she would never forgive him.

Her heart harder than she ever thought possible, she waved farewell to her husband, he full of confidence that his expedition would be a short and successful one, well supported by good men like John Lambert and George Monck, Charles Fleetwood, a humble man but good general, Robert Lilburne, a man more loyal to Cromwell than his ranting Leveller of a brother, and Oliver's own cousin Edward Whalley.

But for all these good men, Elizabeth knew the fear and foreboding of any wife seeing her husband off to war. And she knew that the Scots could be more formidable and obdurately warlike than the Irish had ever been.

Lettie's face was flushed. Ragged strands of pale hair had escaped from the servant's linen cap as she raced back to the Cockpit. They had far more servants now but she still enjoyed doing the shopping whenever possible, lingering a little on a fine day. Today was fine, but she couldn't reach home quickly enough.

She found Lady Cromwell in the kitchen with Mrs Pearson arranging the evening meal. As the wife of the Lord General her mistress would often have important and interesting guests to dinner – people like the beautiful and elegant Frances Lambert, wife of the handsome Colonel John Lambert, and just lately Lord Herbert, son of Lord Worcester. Lord Herbert had his eye on Lady Mary Cromwell. A young man of wit and charm, even Lettie felt her simple heart leap at the sight of him. At this moment, however, far more important matters filled her head.

'My lady, you should see!' she burst out.

Unceremoniously dumping her basket on the kitchen table, she was stopped by Mrs Pearson. 'Not there, dolt! Over there.'

Without taking her eyes from her mistress, Lettie transferred the basket and began unloading leeks, onions, custard apples, and dabs. 'Everyone in Butlers the fishmonger was talking about it.'

'About what?' asked her mistress absently, still checking her list.

'Dunbar, my lady. The Lord Lieutenant . . . No, he's the Lord General now, ain't he?'

'Dunbar?' Lady Cromwell looked directly at her maid.

'In Scotland, my lady. Lord General Cromwell has routed them Scots at Dunbar. A great victory.'

'When was this, Lettie?'

'I don't rightly know, my lady. I was in Butlers when a woman asked for some herring in a Scots accent. The customers jeered at her and she ran out crying. It was said a messenger stopped a coach to tell a passenger of the Scottish being put to flight. He said the news was being taken to Whitehall.'

'No one has been here with such news.'

'I 'spects it will be relayed to you properly soon enough, my lady.'

Within minutes a messenger had arrived, retelling Lettie's garbled news, this time with an official seal to it. Betty, who was staying at the Cockpit while John was in London on business over some plans for a building, anxiously regarded her mother.

'You must prepare yourself for a stream of callers offering you their congratulations,' she said cautiously, aware of her mother's badly disguised dislike of entertaining.

'Lord Herbert will no doubt stop by to add his,' said Mary excitedly.

Her mother gave her a knowing smile. 'No doubt, he being a guest at my table tonight. And a most entertaining one to be sure.'

'He entertains Mall well enough,' laughed Betty.

Listening to them, Frances felt her thoughts turn sour. No one was quite sure exactly when Lord Herbert had been introduced to the family. Betty said it had been at a dinner given by Mrs Lambert. Mama was certain they'd first met him at Sir Thomas and Lady Widdrington's home. Whatever, he was paying a great deal of attention to Mary and Mama seemed ready to encourage it.

Remembering how sharply her own association with Jeremiah White had been terminated, how could she not help having sour thoughts? She had never heard another word from him since – as if Papa had buried him somewhere never to be found. Wherever he was, did he ever think of her? Or had he forgotten her entirely? He could even be married by now. It was possible Papa might even have been at the root of a marriage. The thought made her heart as heavy as lead. And here was Mall allowed to receive overtures and still only fifteen. She wasn't jealous of Mary, but the way Mama was pushing that young man at her was almost vulgar.

'I'm not so far off being ready for suitors,' she said loudly, but no one seemed to be listening.

Later she taxed Mary on it. 'I like him well enough,' she said when Frances asked if she had any loving regard for him. 'He's good company. He is amusing and amiable.'

'And if Papa were to arrange a marriage contract?'

'I should be agreeable, I think. He is very wealthy.' Beyond that she refused to be drawn out on the subject of love.

It wasn't jealousy, Frances told herself, but concern for Mary that prompted her to write to Papa urging him not to press any marriage contract until Mary had declared love for Lord Herbert. She didn't tell Mary about her letter in case she thought her interfering, and perhaps it was just as well, for Papa chose not to refer to it in his tender reply to her.

* * *

For the next two months, news coming out of Scotland provided stimulating conversation at Lady Cromwell's table. That was a great relief to her. She had never considered herself a good host. Brought up to a simpler life, she was a poor conversationalist with highly bred people. 'When your father was but a junior Member of Parliament,' she told Betty, 'I much enjoyed cooking for friends. Now I cook not at all. I am not much given to all this grandeur.'

Betty could only make a show of sympathy. As a daughter of the Lord General, life was exciting, London's fashionable society thrusting aside the old Puritan ways. Spending less and less time in Northampton, she was a constant companion of Frances Lambert, whose taste in fine clothes she copied as far as her purse allowed. In fine fabrics of pretty colours, Betty let her softly rounded shoulders go bare, wore her bodice low, did her hair in ringlets bunched at the sides with ribbons and bows of silk and velvet, and sported little fans; she even had a tiny star-shaped patch on her cheek in the new fashion creeping in. Flitting from one social event to another, her energy sometimes worried her mother, knowing how delicate her health was.

Elizabeth wrote to Oliver for his advice, and not only concerning Betty but Richard as well. He and Dorothy were also frequent visitors to London, and he behaved as though money fell straight from heaven into his lap. Just lately, however, he was looking harassed, so much so that she approached him about it just after Christmas while Doll was writing letters in the rooms they occupied at the Cockpit when they were in London. His reply dismayed her.

'I am broke,' he stated flatly. 'And in debt.'

'That's impossible!' she cried in alarm. 'You spend so freely.'

Elizabeth stared up at him from the chair on which she sat in her withdrawing room – an uncomfortable, rambling room like so many of the rooms in this echoing mausoleum of a place – and noted the wryness of his beautiful smile.

'Why not?' he answered her. 'What I spend is a tiny portion of what I owe. Were I to save like a miser it wouldn't be anywhere near enough to pay my debts. I might as well have the pleasure of what there is for the little while remaining to me.'

'But you have a fine farm.'

'It doesn't pay. One needs capital to expand. Without it . . .' He let his eyes roam to the two liveried servants lighting the candles against the gathering dusk. 'All very well for established squires like Doll's father, with tradesmen jostling to lend money to such creditable men. They did the same to me at first, but not now. Tradesmen are a man's downfall, you know.'

She couldn't even raise an answering smile to his poor jest. 'You have to blame your reputation, Richard. You should have thought of this before you began so carelessly throwing money to the winds. Few are eager to lend money unless certain of repayment and certainty of interest. As to creditors, you are the son of the Lord General of the Commonwealth Army.'

'That makes little difference to creditors,' Richard chuckled bitterly, arousing a small prickle of anger in his mother.

'The difference is that by your debts you are bringing your father's name into disrepute, that is what I am saying. He is a man of principle. He seeks no fortune except for his country. He asks only enough for his needs, which he conducts moderately, unlike you, Dick. He's honest in his dealings and campaigns alike, and every man knows where he stands with him.'

Seeing his lips quirking a little, she rose to her feet. 'You may smile, Richard! I've no wish to see any of his children bring him down by their own disgrace. I will be writing to ask him what is to be done. It is possible he'll settle your debts for you and so see you able to raise your head again. We shall see.'

It had not been easy bothering Oliver with family problems. As she saw it, he had enough to contend with in dealing with a powerful Scottish army in the depths of a harsh Scottish winter.

Edinburgh had allowed his entry amicably enough, but the castle on its rock had remained impregnable under bombardment, finally coming to satisfactory terms of surrender only through betrayal by its commander. The north of the country, however, was made of sterner stuff, continuing to repel his efforts even to the crowning of the young Charles Stuart at Scone on the first of January.

Even so, Elizabeth hopefully awaited Oliver's reply regarding his wayward son. When none came she assumed that bad weather had prevented her letter reaching him. But in February came a report that he'd fallen gravely ill from the severe conditions that had already claimed hundreds of his soldiers. Her reaction was spontaneous.

'I must go to him. It is my duty as his devoted wife.'

It was John Claypole, with his quiet common sense, who persuaded her to listen to reason. 'The snow lies heavy in Scotland,' he told her. 'No coach would get through. You'd have to travel on horseback in conditions not fit for a trooper much less a woman of tender upbringing. It'll take not just a few days but many weeks to go a hundred miles.'

'It is my duty,' she persisted.

'And if your life were put in jeopardy – the biting cold claim you as it has many a strong soldier – while your husband by God's grace regained his health, his very soul would leave him. For you are his beloved wife.'

She twisted her hands together. 'He must imagine I've deserted him.'

'He'd not be so self-seeking,' Claypole said, 'and were he to know of your intentions he would say your prayers are more valuable to him at this moment. The Lord is with him. He will not fail either of you.'

Seeing the wisdom of it, she prayed night and day and recommended as many people as possible to do likewise, even to publishing her wishes. Well into March, prayers for Cromwell's health were on the lips of everyone not of Royalist sympathies, whose own prayers were more for his death. By the beginning of April it was evident who had won, as the Lord General recovered.

To Elizabeth's joy a letter came from his valet, Jean Duret, dated April 1651, which she read aloud to her family.

'Monsieur Duret says your father took his rest very well on the night of Tuesday last and has done so every night since. He says your father is sensible in his own judgement and in Doctor Goddard's, and also has a better stomach and grows daily stronger. Monsieur Duret says that during his illness he would take nourishment from none but his valet, who has devotedly nursed him, gaining his reward in seeing your father well again.'

Putting the letter aside, she added, 'We shall pray that the next we receive will be in your father's own hand. Then truly he'll be recovered.'

But when it came, it wasn't the happiest of letters, criticising some of his family, Elizabeth included. It began well enough, asking her to assure Dick and Doll of his love and prayers and enquiring if the child did well. It thanked his two youngest daughters for their loving letters. It said how deeply he was moved that Bridget was making a great impression in Ireland with her piety, and that his son Henry was also much crying to God. Then without warning the tone turned sour, making Elizabeth's lips grow tight as she read what he called her folly in allowing Lord Herbert too often into her home.

> You must be fully aware that a sum of money was granted me some five years ago by Parliament for my unwearied and faithful service, and that the money was raised from the estates of the Marquess of Worcester, a Papist and a Royalist. Were you not suspicious of Lord Herbert, who is that man's son? That he had wormed his way into your house in hope of recovering those estates by courting our daughter Mary? I would beseech you no more to entertain the man, and further would beseech you to see me in the matter of any future alliance between Mary and whatever other young man takes her eye.

In tears Elizabeth consulted Betty, who had been criticised the least. 'I can't imagine how your father came to know about Lord Herbert. I did not intend to make any secret about it, for I saw the young man as an open enough person, hardly a Royalist for all his father had been. It didn't seem important enough to bother your father, and later, he being so gravely ill, we were taken up more with fear for him. Now he blames me for encouraging the man, even accusing me of concealment.'

In her mother's boudoir, Betty put her arm about her as her mother wept bitterly in relaying even more censure. 'Your father desires I relay his profound displeasure of Richard's debts. He points out to me – *to me* – that Richard's pleasure-seeking should be discouraged when your father's own men lie bleeding and breathing out their last. As though Richard's debts are *my* fault! I've asked your father's advice and received only admonition.'

'He has been ill,' Betty excused with her willingness

to see good in everybody, 'and far away from us and has misinterpreted your letter.'

It only made Elizabeth weep all the more. 'Even you he rebukes, his most sweet-natured of daughters. He reminds you, Betty, beware of worldly vanities and worldly company, to which he suspects you of being too partial.'

She felt her daughter's comforting arm fall away. Betty made no effort to defend herself although it was obvious she knew what he was referring to – her love of fine clothes and fashionable society.

'It isn't fair,' Elizabeth consoled her, but after that Betty grew quiet and reserved and not long afterwards returned to Norborough, leaving her mother full of guilt for having consulted Oliver in the first place.

It was even worse relaying his disapproval of Dick – as a consequence he and Dorothy stayed away as summer wore on, leaving her alone with her two youngest girls.

The Scottish campaign was meant to have been a swift one but was delayed by the Lord General suffering another bout of sickness. He was in terrible pain from a kidney stone, and even Parliament was alarmed, sending two of their most eminent physicians. Although he was recovering, he was still far from fit, and it seemed the Army would be in Scotland yet another year.

Many of Elizabeth's friends, including the vivacious Mrs Lambert, closed up their homes to make the long hazardous journey to join their husbands.

Elizabeth's house became silent, but still smarting from his letter, she flatly told Frances and Mary, 'I will not assist your father.' Both were itching to see that strange country, but she was adamant. 'I would have a little time to myself. That fashionable company seems bent only on being first with the latest hairstyle and the finest dress. I hear Mrs Lambert has sent all the way back to London for

French lawn.' Her voice rang bitterly as she said this. 'Even Colonel Lambert must have hats from France and boots of Spanish leather and must drink only the best Canary sack. I'd rather my own company until your father returns.'

'It's so boring here now,' pined Frances out of her mother's hearing as she and Mall took the warm July air in the garden for want of something better to do. 'Everyone having a wonderful time in Scotland.'

Perched on a low wall, Mary swung her legs beneath a plain dress, with no reason to wear anything brighter. Frances, also plainly dressed, sitting on the lawn aimlessly plucking tender grass shoots to nibble their sweet stems, glanced up at her sister.

'Do you remember Mr White?' she asked.

'Vaguely,' murmured Mary without interest.

'I wonder, will we ever see him again? Although by now he is most likely married.'

'Lord Herbert no longer comes here either. I can't think why.'

Frances cast her a sidelong glance. Papa must have taken note of her letter in his own peculiar way, saying nothing but making his own enquiries, for it wasn't long afterwards that Lord Herbert's visits stopped. Mama gave no answer for it, but from the way she behaved it seemed she might already have the answer. Had she received orders from Papa to discourage him?

Frances felt a twinge of satisfaction in not being the only one whose hopeful suitor had been surreptitiously warned off, felt not quite so alone. At the same time she felt dreadful that her letter had been the instrument of Lord Herbert's banishment. She wished she hadn't brought up the subject of Jeremiah White.

'Do you miss Lord Herbert?' she asked, hoping for reassurance that it had not affected her. To her dismay Mary grew angry.

'Why should I miss him? I shan't pine for him as you did your silly Mr White. Moping about the house. And you still do. Were Mr White to walk into this garden right now, you'd welcome him with open arms. He left with not a word to anyone. And that rude Lord Herbert has done exactly the same. If he comes again to this house I for one shall not receive him.' With that she slid off the wall and ran into the house, leaving Frances to consider the consequences of what she'd done.

Leaning from an upper window of Whitehall Palace, Frances watched the procession going by. All her family, with the exception of Henry and the Iretons, were watching the Lord General come home in triumph. On this beautiful September morning all of London seemed to be going wild with delight for the man who had defeated Charles Stuart at Worcester.

A few weeks earlier it had been a different story, when everyone had trembled at the news of the Scottish-crowned Charles and his army riding southward towards the Capital. In panic they'd dug ditches around the city, accusing Cromwell of laxity and ill leadership in letting him slip through his fingers to England. How could they know he'd deliberately left the way open, fooling Charles into thinking he'd left the border unguarded.

The bait had been taken and when Charles had cleared the border, Cromwell, whose army had gone north, turned and came swiftly after him, marching parallel to him down the east of England. Lambert's cavalry had joined up with Major General Harrison to snap at Charles Stuart's rear while Colonel Fleetwood, having returned to London after Dunbar, moved up from the south with a fresh army. Thus disappointed that more Royalists had not joined him and with his own men exhausted, Charles had found his army trapped in the narrow streets and alleyways of Worcester by some thirty-five thousand men and militia.

Two thousand Royalists died, piled up in the alleys. Cromwell's losses had been two hundred. He took nine thousand prisoners, the rest escaping back to Scotland while Charles Stuart was reported trying to find his way back to France, alone and utterly defeated.

Cromwell was now the brilliant strategist, the great leader of men, the unbeatable commander, on his way to Westminster amid almost hysterical cheers and volley upon volley of great and small shot, the Lord's work done.

Frances heard the joyful shots in the distance, excitement mounting as she shouted to Mary leaning from the next window, 'Mall! Such a crowd!'

Below her was a swaying checkerboard of white linen bonnets and black, tall-crowned hats, with brighter splashes of colour seen in the plumed hats of the more flamboyant in the crowd. Everywhere people were hanging from windows, those below calling up to ask if they could see anything of the approaching procession. Every window of Whitehall Palace was filled with relatives and privileged guests of the Cromwells, their maids and servants, their children and their nurses.

Three windows along, Frances saw the family of Jean Duret. Nursing her father during his first terrible bouts of illness in Edinburgh, Duret had succumbed to total exhaustion and had died. In gratitude for his devotion, Papa had honoured his valet's dying wish that he help his kin. He'd brought the Duret family – his mother, his sister and nephews – over from France and Mama had welcomed them into her home, to Madame Duret's deep-felt thanks. Frances and Mary, as the only ones to understand the language, acted as translators, and although Madame Duret found English difficult, her daughter and grandsons had picked it up very well during the year.

Seeing Frances gazing at them, Madame Duret waved to her. Frances was about to wave back when she noticed the movement of the crowd below becoming more urgent. There came a fanfare of trumpets, growing louder by the second, and the beating of drums, the cheers rising in waves like flocks of disturbed pigeons.

'He's here!' Mary was shrieking. Everyone was straining to lean as far as they could from their windows as swinging into Whitehall came pipers and trumpeters and drummers, then foot soldiers – columns of them.

Buff-coated, pot-helmeted, they marched with shouldered muskets, in step to the vibrant drum roll and rat-tat-too of side drums. Following them were the pikemen, almost hidden by a forest of shouldered pikes. Then dragoons with more pipe and drum. The noise was deafening. Then, coming into view, Cromwell himself in full armour and riding a deep-chested, chestnut mount. Mary was shrieking herself hoarse, with everyone waving and calling out.

One hand holding the reins, the Lord General waved and doffed his befeathered hat to the crowds in recognition of their cheers, and as he moved on past the windows of Whitehall Palace, he looked up at those above him with an extra salute of his hat by whirling it about his head like a schoolboy.

'He is thinner,' Elizabeth called to Betty, her concern for his health showing even over her joy.

'We will make him fat again!' Betty called back.

Passing directly beneath his family, his face beamed up at them; his lips moved, but the din drowned out his words. Surrounded by his noble captains, his cousin Edward Whalley, John Lambert and Thomas Harrison, the gentlemanly Charles Fleetwood, the portly and heavy-featured George Monck, Cromwell rode at the head of his cavalry like a king.

In the glorious September sunshine, breast- and back-plates glittered, curled bright feathers of the jaunty hats bounced bravely to the spirited step of their mounts, points of white collars – knotted only when in battle – flapping loosely at each step. Harnesses jangled. It was enough to stimulate the most retiring soul as the crowd yelled its welcome.

'It's a sight!' Mary squealed, but Frances had her eyes on a smaller, more sombrely dressed body of men coming into sight positioned between the rear of the cavalry and the clustering Members of Parliament. They rode black-cloaked, black-hatted, the chaplains and ministers. And among them one face held her gaze – the smooth youthful features of Mr Jeremiah White.

Frances felt her heart give an enormous leap. 'Oh, praise be to God! Papa has forgiven him after all,' she cried out, but everyone was cheering so much that no one heard her.

Seven

1652

'I can hardly believe this is all ours!'

Having waltzed around this small deserted room in Hampton Court Palace, Mary sank out of breath into an ornate chair.

Together they'd run through an endless maze of corridors, passages, galleries, peeking into rooms, negotiating narrow stairways, venturing into state bedrooms, had skipped breathlessly down the grand staircase, blinking at all the rich hangings and paintings. They had flitted across large open courts where people strolled, had crept through tiny deserted courtyards hemmed in by high, small-windowed, red brick buildings that all but shut out the sunlight.

Their footsteps had echoed with those of the servants hurrying along stone passages that led to the kitchens. In the great kitchen they had stood awed by the huge fireplace seventeen feet across. Kitchen staff carrying trays of hot food and armfuls of yet-to-be-cooked food glanced in surprise at the prettily dressed young daughters of Oliver Cromwell himself.

In the high-vaulted wine cellar they had been chased out by a dark-bearded man in a stained leather apron, ordering the dainty young ladies back to their own domain above the stairs and not to be bothering his staff.

Doing as they were told, Frances and Mary found

themselves confronted by the overwhelming dimensions of the great hall, its hammer-beam ceiling soaring so high above them that the guests standing around in conversation were dwarfed by it all. They were told on enquiring that the height was sixty feet.

Hardly waiting to thank the heavily bewigged and extremely fat little man for his information, they'd skipped away, ending up out of breath with laughter in this exquisitely panelled room furnished with an oak chest, a little round table and two finely upholstered chairs upon which they now threw themselves.

The little room, cosy compared with much of the rest of the place, had once been the closet of Cardinal Wolsey before he was obliged to hand his beautiful palace over to his king. Neither of the girls knew whose closet it had been but they knew the whole palace had once belonged to Henry VIII and had now been handed to their own father in grateful acknowledgement of his victories, all the pictures and furnishings that had previously been sold on the death of King Charles hurriedly bought back for its new owner.

'All this is ours,' Mary repeated. 'I think Papa must be so proud.'

'Not all of it is ours,' Frances pointed out as she fanned her face with her hand. It was warm for late October, and with all that running it felt even warmer. 'Mama said that Papa had been offered a grand suite of rooms here, but neither she nor Papa really wanted them.'

'That's silly,' scoffed Mary. 'Why not?'

Frances shrugged. 'You know Papa. He cares little for grandeur. He even declined entirely at first.'

'Well, he has now accepted, else we wouldn't be here.'

'We're not to live here,' Frances put in. 'We'll continue to live in London. Papa says it's more convenient to Westminster. From now on he is to be a Member of Parliament instead of a soldier.' She sat up to regard her sister, her eyes glowing. 'Think of it, Mall. He will never be going away again.'

But Mary wasn't interested about their father hanging up his sword. 'Then why are we here today if not to view our new home?'

'It's to be a retreat for him. It was Betty who suggested we all view it today while we have a chance to.'

Mary got up sharply and went to the tiny leaded casement window that looked out on to a narrow courtyard. 'Papa does everything his favourite daughter asks of him. Even coming to a place he has no intention of living in permanently.'

'That's not fair, Mall!' scolded Frances. Mary could be so silly at times that she often felt the older of the two. 'You can't blame Betty.'

'I'm not blaming her,' said Mary, continuing to stare out of the window. 'It merely seems that he bows to her every whim, yet he frowns on anything *we* ask of him.'

Frances knew to what she was referring. The banishment of Lord Herbert still rankled with Mary, though whether she longed for him Frances doubted. Mary hadn't known that aching loss she herself had suffered at Jeremiah White's unexplained disappearance, nor the pent-up excitement she now knew at his being here not far away from her; that she might come upon him at any time; that their eyes might meet and she read in their warmth that message she longed to see.

Papa wasn't all stern. He had brought Jeremiah back. 'Papa gives us all he can,' she said, her heart dancing.

'It isn't what he *gives* us.' Mary turned to look at Frances, a knowing expression on her face. 'It's what he *disallows* us. Such as advising Mama not to receive Lord Herbert any more.'

Frances stared at her. Did she know about the letter she'd written to Papa? 'How did . . . How did you know?' In danger of giving herself away, she stopped her wayward tongue behind hurriedly compressed lips.

'Oh, come, Frankie,' returned Mary. 'I'm not such a dolt as not to have put two and two together on such an abrupt termination of his visits. I expect Mama, in all innocence, wrote to Papa of him and he didn't approve. I know why too. Because Lord Herbert is said to have Royalist connections.'

'But you never appeared too put out by his going. You even said you would not receive him if he ever came calling again.'

Heartily relieved at no blame being laid at her door, Frances was unprepared for her sister's violent response.

'Who are you to say I wasn't put out?' Mary looked about ready to burst into tears. 'I had the highest regard for him, Royalist or not. I might have come to love him with all my heart had he not been ordered to absent himself from me. It was *assumed* he was planning to entice my affections for his own ends, and it infuriates me beyond all endurance. How *dare* Papa order him away with no word to me or a chance for him to vindicate himself. I was hurt more than words could say. And you speak of my complacency? Can you not recall your own feelings when Mr White was sent away?'

Frances' first reaction was to retort that *she* hadn't had to wait for love to bloom – it had burst into flower at her very first sight of Mr White.

Caution froze the retort. It had been a month since his return and her only glimpse of him had been during the homecoming procession. He was still in London, she knew, but until she came face to face with him again, he able to speak with her and make his feelings known – if he still fostered any – she must hold her tongue lest her imprudence reach unsympathetic ears and he again be posted. She shrugged and remained silent.

* * *

For all Mary's regret at not residing permanently at Hampton Court, the Cockpit was far cosier on a wet and blustery November evening. Frances regretted not being there for totally different reasons. With Jerry White ordered to remain there, she hardly saw him. When she did, it had been at a distance or with others around perhaps to see how her eyes followed him everywhere, and, she was sure, his followed her. Her heart ached when Papa left to return here, mostly at Mama's insistence, unhappy with the vastness of that more stately residence.

With the parlour curtains drawn, Frances and Mary sat before the blazing hearth embroidering samplers for their bedrooms while Mama sat at her little writing table composing a letter to Bridget.

Frances let her eyes wander from her labour to conjure up Jerry's image in the flames – such a beautiful image. The image grew misty and she realised it was her eyes that were misty. Were these tears to be noticed by Mama there would be awkward questions unable to be answered. Frances breathed in deeply, stretched her back, and forced her mind to think of other things.

'Shouldn't Papa be home soon?' she queried. 'He's been in the House all day. What does Parliament have to talk about to keep them so long?'

Lettie came into the room and with a small respectful bob enquired whether Mrs Pearson should keep supper warm or serve it now. 'Seeing as there's no other guests at the table tonight,' she finished.

Elizabeth glanced up from writing to consult the little pinnacled silver clock at her elbow. It showed six o'clock. 'Tell Mrs Pearson a quarter of an hour should see your master home. Else he'd have sent a messenger to say he would be delayed.' At which Lettie bobbed again and hurried away.

Almost to the quarter hour carriage wheels crunched to a halt in the main yard, the throaty cries of the driver bringing stable hands, grooms, equerries and household servants, one of whom hurried off to Elizabeth's plain and humble little parlour set to one side in this great rambling place to announce that the master had arrived home.

Hurriedly and with some excitement, Frances and Mary threw aside their embroidery and ran to the great hall as their father's house manager, Maidstone, opened the main entrance door to him – and a damp gust of wind – before it was hastily closed again.

Pulling off his hat, spattered with rain in the dash from coach door to house door, Cromwell slapped it heartily against his thigh and together with his cloak and leather gauntlets tossed it to Maidstone. His inharmonious voice filled the hall, bringing it instantly to life.

'A fine night, is it not, Maidstone?' With his flat guffaw, he turned to his daughters, who appeared awed by the rain still dripping from his cloak on to the flagstones. 'Lead me to a fire and a warming supper.' He threw a jovial arm about each of their shoulders as though they were children. 'How are my little wenches?'

Frances shrank from the chill of his garments. 'You are still damp, Papa,' she complained, but he gave another loud raucous laugh.

'A mere feather in the cap, little one.' He still called her that for all she was near the same height as he. 'A trifling dribble to one who has been in a day's downpour with no scrap of shelter. I feel no discomfort but what a good hearty meal will cure.'

He released them as their mother came hurrying into the hall, Lady Cromwell signalling to Lettie – who was scurrying behind her, as ever her shadow lest she be dismissed in preference to all these grand servants that surrounded her mistress these days – to alert Mrs Pearson of the master's return. It was to Lettie's constant relief that Lady Cromwell still favoured her two trusted servants of long standing, her simple style declaring the fewer servants around her the better.

'Ah, Joan, my dear!' thundered Cromwell, using his term of endearment for his wife – one he alone used in that vein, his enemies using the name with contempt for her simple origins. He bent and kissed her offered cheek then straightened up. 'Lead the way to the supper table, my dear. I am famished. What a day we have had! Things have gone very well at the House today.'

'I'm glad,' she said simply as he led the way to the small dining hall.

In this cosy setting, where voices fell muffled on soft drapes and furnishings, Oliver relaxed, helping himself to mutton broth from a steaming tureen which Lettie had brought to the table.

'The most heartening news, my dear,' he stated, chewing on a piece of mutton. 'Limerick has surrendered to Ireton. At last, after so long holding out, the country is finally and totally subdued. God bless our noble Ireton for his great work there. The Lord of Hosts has truly been with us.'

'Does it mean Bridget and her husband will be coming home?'

Frances could project no enthusiasm into her enquiry. The idea of her ever disapproving brother-in-law residing in this house wasn't an appealing one, and Bridget, having become too pious for words whilst in Ireland, would be a trial to her if not to them all.

'Not so, my little wench,' said her father, almost sadly. 'Ireland still has need of him there. He is a fine commander and I have none able enough to replace him, as much as I would have him and Bridget and their sweet children here at my side.'

She thought he had heard her relieved exhalation as his

smile faded and he put his spoon down quietly. But his expression had become pensive.

'I should like for us all to pray for our dear Ireton. It is said he is somewhat unwell. A chill, we are told, from which he has derived a fever of sorts. Of course, it is of small consequence to a man of action, but he and his little family are so far away from us that we can give no succour except in our prayers. The Lord will see him well soon enough, for in Ireland he is about the Lord's work. But it is irksome for a man such as he to be put to bed by a chill.'

The twisted smile – one that nature had deemed never to be other than his – now returned. 'I will instruct my chaplains to pray earnestly this coming Sunday for his swift recovery.'

With this he returned heartily to the business of eating, leaving his youngest daughter's heart to flutter with excitement at the utterance of the word 'chaplains'.

Cromwell chose the favourite of his chaplains, John Owen, to give the first sermon, with two lesser ministers in attendance for good measure. 'All will be well now,' he stated confidently, with everyone in total agreement as they departed the meeting – everyone but Frances, whose mind had become a delicious whirl since the final sermon.

That last, the shortest, and by far the most brilliant of all three, had been delivered with a good deal of hesitation and stumbling on words from the very moment that he had seen her sitting there in the congregation, his eyes hardly leaving her face except to search for a lost place in his notes. She in turn had been struck motionless, her gaze mesmerised, her cheeks growing hotter and hotter, her hands growing damper and damper, and she had been unable to think of nothing but Jeremiah White's most exquisite countenance.

Since then, wherever she went, she could sense him nearby. But as a daughter of Cromwell there was no way in which she could make open enquiries as to his young chaplain's whereabouts. All she could do was wait in hope that he would make the first approach – if he dared. The waiting was a prolonged agony.

But any meeting, whether by chance or design, was destined to take second place to the news that arrived, stunning the whole family, the whole nation. News taking a week or more to reach them even by the swiftest routes from Ireland, their prayers for Bridget's husband, Ireton, had come too late.

By the time Oliver's chaplains had called upon the Lord for Ireton's deliverance, he was already dead. Plague having broken out in the town of Limerick, it had claimed him as one of its victims and the raising of another Lazarus had apparently not been in the mind of the Almighty. The terrible news not arriving until the beginning of December, and Christmas not being a time for merrymaking in the Puritan calendar, the days of midwinter were turned into a season of mourning.

It was a sad and silent assembly that saw Henry Ireton's widow arrive in London, her husband's remains having been taken across the Irish Sea to Bristol on the seventeenth of December. A slow and laborious journey from Bristol, with the wagon bearing his corpse being continually bogged down in the rutted winter roads, took two weeks, Bridget having to rest frequently at lodging houses. The ordeal brought her down woefully.

Ireton's body lay in state at Somerset House; Bridget and her brother Henry, who had made the journey with her from Ireland, went to Whitehall with their parents, the carriage blinds drawn against morbid spectators. For the most part their route was lined by solemn onlookers, but as they neared Westminster one or two catcalls were hurled from the crowd.

All this time Bridget had held herself remarkably well despite the terrible ordeal of her lonely and despairing journey from Ireland. Behind her widow's weeds none knew if tears fell or not. Then from out of the crowd came an isolated, high-pitched jeering and without any prior warning the woman of strength was at that moment transformed into a distraught child. The taut self-control snapped and with a strangled coughing sob, Bridget collapsed against her mother, her face buried in the folds of her mourning.

'Why?' A shuddering, drawn-out plea, like the timeless question of all who are bereaved, tore at the hearts of those in the carriage with her as her mother hugged the weeping girl to her.

'Royalists!' Cromwell's voice grated his hatred of the beasts without feelings who could mock a woman, any woman, in her grief.

'We do not know why,' murmured Elizabeth, her hand on her child, her woman's instinct probing far deeper than that of any man's. 'Only our Lord can know that, my dear child. He who cried out the very same word whilst upon His cross – "*Why* hast thou forsaken me?" – can give you the answer, and comfort, for He knows why.'

Her arms encircling the weakened woman in the form of a protective cloak, the men looked on, awkward and confused, knowing that they had been found wanting.

'There is nothing to be gained,' Oliver ventured with the masculine inadequacy of a man confounded. 'It will not bring our dear son back . . .'

He was stopped by his wife's withering glance. 'My dear, look to your own form of grief and leave women to theirs!' After which she bent her head again to her daughter, leaving him crestfallen, at a loss to cope with the terrible, muffled sounds of despair that only the bereaved can make. Accustomed to dealing with men who guarded their pain and sorrow before the company of their own sort – if perhaps not before the opposite sex, whose ability to mother them often made babies of them – he held his own grief tightly within himself. He had lost too much – a dear son-in-law and friend with whom he had been as close as a brother from the very commencement of their conflict with the King. His loss clawed at his chest as cruel as a knife being turned in the flesh. But blubbering aloud did not bring Ireton back so he prayed silently instead, for strength, strength for himself, for them all, that they would trust more in the Lord, through whose great strength they would all endeavour to face this ordeal as the carriage took them slowly back towards home and sanctuary from the gawking of the public.

By the time the coach reached the Cockpit, Bridget had control of herself again. Shielded from the crowd that had gathered about the entrance, her mother to one side of her, her brother to the other, her father behind them responding little to the tentative and ragged cheer that arose out of respect for his presence, Bridget's back was straight, her face unseen behind heavy black veils, but her head was high, giving none the satisfaction of witnessing her grief. Seeing her action, Oliver's face reflected his pride in his stalwart daughter, in all his brave family as they made their way up the steps to the building.

'How can they be so heartless?' Frances had protested fiercely against the catcalls. By March she found herself repeating those words, this time against insults not from strangers but from those who should have possessed more common decency.

In March Ireton was given a state funeral, the noblest that Cromwell could devise with the blessing of Parliament.

With pomp as magnificent as any given to a prince, the body was borne in solemn procession to Westminster Abbey to be laid to rest in King Henry VII's Chapel. If there were jeers, they were drowned out by the deep protracted roll of drums that accompanied the procession along the whole route – a very different beat to the previous year when Cromwell had come home in triumph from Scotland. In closed coaches followed the entire Cromwell family, and even the senior Elizabeth Cromwell, Oliver's mother. In her eighty-seventh year and so frail that a doctor was in attendance, she summoned strength enough to support her sorrowing son though the ordeal took much out of her.

Throughout the entire ceremony Bridget was inconsolable; gone was the upright, stoic posture, the highly held head, when she walked through the crowd gathered outside her father's home. To Frances, seeing her now, it seemed she had finally run out of reserves and all that was left was her poor racked body, so hidden in deepest mourning it was difficult to distinguish her shape much less her face. For once, Frances felt genuine sorrow for her, even vague regret for her dead husband, both of whom she'd always found insufferable in their piety and overbearing censorship of others they deemed less pious. Now she looked on a woman so distressed that John Owen, deputised to read the sermon, feared to even refer to her as the widow or the bereaved or the relic lest she break down totally.

Frances couldn't help thinking as she listened to him that a man like John Owen, able to reduce his congregation to trembling wrecks with his promise of damnation for their shortcomings, could be so considerate to poor Bridget, much as a father might. Yet even he couldn't soothe away her sense of loss for all his praising her husband's abilities, comparing him to the biblical Daniel, 'seeing all earthly events as divine dispensation unlike those who like swine followed acorns beneath the tree and not one looking up to the tree to see from whence they fell.' In truth the text made matters worse, until Bridget's uncontrollable sobbing could be heard throughout the Abbey, inducing tears from the whole assembly.

But there was more to add to her distress as the days went by, the first incident stemming from an unknown wag who thought it fit to corrupt the achievement to Ireton that was placed over the gate of Somerset House where he had lain in state. The motto ran, *Dulce et decorum est pro patria mori*, or 'It was for the good of his country that he died.' Translated by the wit, it became, 'It was good for his country that he died.'

The joke spread among Ireton's enemies, adding to Bridget's already deep distress. But even that wasn't as hurtful or as cruel as that which was done to her some weeks later, obviously with more intent than innocence.

Still in her mourning, Bridget's face was streaked with tears as she, Mary and Frances came home in her coach after taking some much needed air. The coachman had been ordered to whip up the horses so that she could get home as soon as possible to collapse into her alarmed mother's arms.

'How could she?' she burst out, all but falling out of the vehicle as her mother came hurrying to see why her daughter's coach had pulled up with such violence. 'To throw my pain and sorrow into my face.'

Between them they helped the overwrought woman up to Elizabeth's boudoir, where they would not be interrupted, and there sat her down on a chair to try to calm her enough to tell her mother what had happened. It was Mary who supplied most of it, she and Frances having been present and witnessed it all.

Mary was nearly as beside herself as Bridget. 'We were strolling in St James's Park,' she related angrily. 'We saw Mrs Lambert on the arm of her husband with several companions. I swear she had seen us from afar – she must have done – but pretended not to. As we drew near, we made ready to bid her good day. At first she didn't look our way, but to those around her she said in a voice loud and clear enough for the entire world to have heard, "Of course you know that Colonel Lambert has been requested to take up the duties of Lord Deputy in Ireland and I daresay he will fulfil them without recourse to so strict a hand as did his predecessor." They were her very words, Mama.'

'And the rest,' urged Bridget, recovering enough to take her hands from her face.

Mary looked uncertainly at her. 'Do you think I ought?'

'You must, for I could never speak the words, although they will be engraved upon my heart to my dying day.'

Drawing in a deep breath and with a pitying look at her older sister, Mary ploughed on, the incident so vividly committed to memory that it could be repeated virtually word for word.

'Still refusing to look our way, she, Mrs Lambert, as though she still hadn't seen us, said, "How terrible the story goes, that as my husband's predecessor lay dying of the plague, he did rave in a fever that he would have *blood and blood and more blood.* How could the man say such a thing, even in a fever?" Then she went on to say, "Of course one cannot always believe such rumours, but knowing how cruelly Ireland was subdued by him . . ." At which point she broke off, pretending to see us for the first time.'

Almost in tears herself, Mary put a hand on Bridget's now trembling shoulder. 'As we passed, she bent her head sweetly towards poor Bridget and said so patronisingly that I could have hit her in full view of everyone present, "Ah, good Mrs Ireton, how pleasant to see you abroad after your sad loss. I trust you are well again?" And on she swept as if the three of us were dust beneath her feet. It was so utterly humiliating, the others looking on to witness her queening it over Bridget, who they were all aware no longer has a place in Ireland through the most unfortunate of circumstances.'

Bridget was weeping afresh, her mother's usually placid face drawn down in fury. 'And what were Colonel Lambert's reactions to all this?' she demanded of Bridget, who could not answer.

It was Frances who answered in her place. 'He looked taken aback. What could he say without the risk of embarrassing his wife in public?'

Her reward for presumptuousness was a censorious glance from her mother. 'Was not *Bridget* embarrassed in public? The woman's a harridan, no less. She has no humility!'

Bending over the crumpled form of her eldest daughter, she held the quaking shoulders with both hands. 'I thank God, my dear, that you had grace enough to resist a retort. It would have made a greater public scene had you done so, and our family would have been shown up.'

'We *have* been shown up,' Bridget sobbed.

'But can feel ourselves blameless.' She began to pull Bridget gently up from the chair at the same time swivelling her head towards her other two daughters. 'Help me assist Bridget to her room. She needs to rest after such a fearful humiliating encounter.'

After they had got Bridget into bed and seen the puffed eyelids close in exhausted sleep, Elizabeth added with quiet deliberation, 'I shall consult your father's advice on this matter.' They knew she would, with the utmost severity; small and reserved though she was, Elizabeth was adept at the quiet word that could bring walls tumbling down.

Eight

Sitting on her sister's bed Frances sipped her warm buttermilk, delaying the time for retiring to her own room, and gazed at Mall.

'Do you think Papa will banish Colonel Lambert?'

Mary regarded her over the rim of her cup before lowering it. 'Just for something his wife said? I doubt it. A man cannot always be responsible for what his silly wife says.'

That was no proper argument. Papa had a habit of banishing all who offended him. He'd sent Jeremiah White away for far less indiscretion. How worse would he handle Colonel Lambert, who had allowed his wife to insult Bridget without so much as lifting a finger to stop her? She put her cup so sharply back down on the little tray that sat near the edge of the bed that the buttermilk slopped on to its surface.

'Do you defend him then? Is it because he is handsome and dresses so finely? If a husband is considered to be responsible for his wife and guide her in everything, so should he take blame for her stupid actions!'

'I would have a man guide me,' said Mary a little wistfully.

Frances regarded her with disdain. 'We are told that man serves God and that woman serves God by serving her husband.' That this reasoning was contrary to her own nature she chose to ignore. There was a point to be made here. 'And he in turn must honour and protect her and be responsible for her conduct,' she hurried on. 'Colonel Lambert did nothing to check his wife that day, so Papa should call on him to apologise for the grief she caused Bridget. Even if he is one of Papa's most valued commanders, Papa should . . . Oh!'

A squeal of consternation put an end to the tirade as her wildly gesticulating hand caught the cup so that milk spilt across the tray on to the polished floor at the side of the bed. Trying to catch it, all she did was knock both cup and tray on to the floor too. Both girls leapt up, Mary's voice high and berating as though glad to see the tables turned on her ranting sister.

'Oh, Frankie! Now see what you've done!'

'It's easily cleaned up.' Frances ran to the door and hurried to the head of the stairs to see a chubby figure crossing the hall below.

'Lettie!' The girl looked up. 'Bring a cloth. We've spilt some milk. Hurry! And don't tell Mother.'

Moments later Lettie was energetically dabbing up the mess. 'One'd think she'd whip you,' she remarked. 'You peeping over them banisters, m'Lady, like you was in terror, anyone'd think your mother a dragon if one didn't know her for such a gentle lady.'

'No one was in terror,' snapped Frances at the stupid girl. 'She has had to bear too many upsets of late without us adding to it.'

'Were I her,' muttered Lettie as she dropped the sopping cloth into the pail she had brought with her, 'I'd have gone and boxed the ears of that Lambert woman, straight I would've.'

'Lettie,' cut in Mary sternly. 'Mind your tongue, if you please.' At which reprimand the girl bit at her lip, mumbled, 'Yes, m'Lady,' and hurried away.

The following day they watched their father closely before he left for the House, but his face was not red with rage nor were his grey eyes glinting with righteous indignation. If anything he appeared at peace with the world.

'Mama couldn't have told him,' said Mary with some disappointment after he had dropped a benign kiss on both their cheeks.

'She must have,' said Frances. 'She would never withhold such a serious incident from him.' Even so, she couldn't wait to ask Mama whether she had or not.

'He has been informed,' was the reply, 'and will no doubt take his own counsel on it when he is ready.'

Frances recalled the way her letter to him had been taken note of, Lord Herbert banished with no word to anyone.

'At the moment,' her mother went on, 'your father has much else on his mind. Parliament takes all his attentions these days.'

'Taking his own counsel,' Frances reported back to Mary.

'Which means it could be ages,' said Mary. 'Think how long it took him to come to a decision to execute King Charles. Every decision Papa has ever made is a battle with him, yet in true battle he is quick and without hesitation, and it is always the right decision. In Parliament he is ever worried and uncertain.'

'Perhaps it isn't Papa but this useless Rump Parliament which is at fault,' Frances mused. It seemed her father was being slowly sucked down into the mire this Parliament was becoming. A hundred Members known as the Rump were all that remained of over two hundred. Its aim supposedly the settlement of the nation, it seemed incapable of settling even itself.

Often sitting five days a week, hardly any business was ever achieved, and her father ranted so much on his return home that no one dared speak to him lest he fly into a rage.

He now had the added burden of antagonism with the Netherlands. With Catholic Spain or France, whose sympathies were with Charles Stuart, it would have been easier for him, but the Dutch were so akin to the English that it seemed nonsensical. A squabble had turned into full conflict – a mere argument over English shipping rights; Dutch herring buses fishing too near English shores; the refusal of the Dutch to dip their topsails and lower ensigns when passing any English squadron, leading to angry exchanges of gunfire until hostilities could only be seen as war – and this silly Parliament at a loss what to do about it.

With her head turned with interest towards politics, Frances listened avidly to all her father came home to inflict upon his family.

'The Rump seems intent on destroying itself with indecision!' he had raged a few days ago, stomping up and down the hall, his harsh flat voice flinging itself against the rafters and the walls. 'I hold it together only by constant argument and debate, the weight of the whole country falling on my shoulders alone.'

No wonder he becomes so unsure at times, thought Frances, recalling his rages. No one but himself to turn to on what best action to take on state matters. Little wonder he is so distant with family problems, leaving Mama to solve them. But she too had her problems. While Bridget was trying to get through the loss of her husband, Dorothy's second child, born January 1652, had been a sickly little thing and had died in April. Given no opportunity to go and console her whilst Bridget was inconsolable, Mama had been pulled this way and that. But Dorothy, feeling the emptiness of her loss, had turned to her husband for comfort and was pregnant again.

'Too soon,' Elizabeth told Oliver. 'That one will be weak too. The more time a woman has between bearing children the stronger will be the next child.'

'Such things are in God's hands,' he remarked. Trying to recuperate from a hectic day in the House, he wanted only to leave women's problems to women. 'A woman cannot dictate when or not she should bear a child. We can only pray for her.'

He seemed to have put the matter of Colonel Lambert completely to one side. Expecting stupendous public retribution being brought on the Lamberts, Frances felt utter disappointment. 'Papa has come to a decision after all,' she told Mary bitterly. 'A decision to do nothing. How poor Bridget must feel I cannot imagine.'

But though the Lamberts continued to walk abroad with their friends, John Lambert as far as anyone knew still in line for the office in Ireland left vacant by Ireton's death, Bridget had begun to recover a little, if not enough to leave the house. She had quite a few callers who sympathised with her over Mrs Lambert's treatment, among them Colonel Charles Fleetwood, who had been a witness to her humiliation in St James's Park.

One Thursday for more than an hour he sat with her and her mother in the little parlour her mother had fashioned for herself. There was a new glow to Bridget's sallow complexion as she plied him with a glass of sherry sack whilst she enjoyed a bowl of tea that Lady Widdrington swore had wonderful uplifting properties for a low spirit.

Seated comfortably on one of the green silk-upholstered chairs whilst the late May sunshine streamed in through the square-paned windows, Charles Fleetwood held the two women's interest with little anecdotes that soon had Bridget laughing as few had heard in a long time – years in fact, for she and her husband had never much laughed. As Fleetwood left, it seemed to her mother that he held Bridget's hand just a little longer than was necessary.

'As I have explained,' he said, ready to take his leave of them, 'I am a widower. As such I know what it is to suffer pangs at the loss of a beloved spouse. Had I been insulted as were you, I'd have lost all self-control. As it is, my dear Mrs Ireton, I commend you on your admirable handling of that deplorable situation in which the lady – if I should call her such – put you. Indeed, you have my heartfelt admiration.'

'That is very kind of you, sir,' said Bridget, almost simpering. But instead of departing he hovered as if loath to leave.

'May I ask one thing of you, Mrs Ireton? May I earnestly ask that you call on my support should you encounter any further slight upon your person? Indeed, I should be most honoured if you could find it in yourself to rely on me for any occasion which you may be at a loss to deal with.'

In reply, Bridget coloured prettily and bowed her head in assent.

Elizabeth Cromwell noticed as they watched him ride off – a straight-backed soldier, resplendent in his colonel's uniform, his befeathered broad-brimmed hat jauntily aslant, gauntletted hands holding the reins high – that Bridget was holding herself proud as any young girl as she looked out upon the world for the first time since her bereavement.

'Charles Fleetwood is a most charming person,' announced Bridget after his having called on her three times in two weeks. The second and third time, her mother had prudently left them alone together in her parlour. Out of Bridget's hearing, Mary consulted Frances.

'Do you think there's something in it?'

'The way she is behaving,' returned Frances, 'I think there must be.'

They stood at the top of the curving staircase, leaning just far enough over the balustrade to see the closed parlour door behind which Bridget and Charles Fleetwood were again sequestered.

'What do you think of him?' asked Frances.

Mary frowned. 'He has a scholarly expression and a proud bearing. His nose is too long and his forehead too high. He must be near forty. Thirty-five at least.'

'Bridget isn't exactly young,' put in Frances. 'Twenty-eight makes her no blushing maiden.'

'She blushes well enough lately,' Mary giggled, but grew suddenly serious. 'Do you think Papa knows of her entertaining him? He is never in the house when Papa comes home. He may well object to such visits.'

For a moment Frances felt a twinge of envy. The man she had turned her eyes to was forbidden to her whereas Bridget was apparently able to entertain this particular male visitor with impunity. 'She is a mature woman,' she said sharply, 'and can no doubt do as she pleases.'

'She is a widow,' reminded Mary. 'As such she is Papa's responsibility. He is so much in the nation's eye these days. The country watches all he and his family do. Publishers of broadsheets are never slow to print what the people wish to read, and make much out of little. What then will they make out of the Lord General's eldest daughter, so recently widowed, entertaining one of his own colonels in his home?'

'How can they know?' scoffed Frances. 'She is the most discreet of persons.'

'Papa has enemies,' said Mary darkly as they made their way down the stairs, having tired of watching the closed parlour door. 'They have keen ears and eyesight. They would bring him down if they could, by whatever means.'

But Frances had a feeling that Bridget, unlike her or Mary, would be the receiver of Papa's blessings in this.

By his fourth visit, Charles Fleetwood was suggesting

that Bridget address him as Charles. He in turn would address her as Bridget. Like a young girl with her first suitor, Bridget readily agreed.

'Papa must know what is passing between them,' Frances said crossly when she heard about it. 'Surely he can't pretend ignorance.'

Within a week of this observation he did indeed call Bridget aside. In the privacy of the parlour where she had so recently entertained Fleetwood, he seated himself in the same chair which Fleetwood would occupy.

With Bridget seated opposite him, he began. 'I understand you have been receiving Colonel Fleetwood.'

Her sharp face remained controlled, her tone dignified, as her steady gaze met his. 'I am of an age and experience of this world and its griefs to conduct myself with sufficient propriety, Father.'

The clear grey eyes studied her for a moment or two, then he smiled and relaxed back in his chair. 'Indeed you are, Biddy, my dear. Though my main interest is to discover what exactly you think of him.'

There was no relaxing on her part. 'He is in every way a gentle and considerate man and of a peaceable spirit.'

'And you – what is the measure of your affection for him? Is there no leaping of the heart when he greets you?'

At last her cold mien broke. 'I have only six months been widowed!'

Her father remained placid. 'And Fleetwood robbed of his own wife a few short weeks after the battle of Worcester, two days before the loss of our dear Ireton.'

'So he has told me.' Her tone became sad. 'Our separate losses so very short a time ago, too soon an affection would be wrong in the Lord's eyes.'

'The Lord forbids love only in incest and adultery and fornication, my dear,' he reminded slowly. 'Your husband is dead . . . No, Bridget, do not weep,' he said as she chewed quickly on her lip and lowered her head as her eyes moistened. 'Charles Fleetwood's wife is at rest in the Lord's arms. What cannot be changed must be accepted.'

Bridget lifted her head and rose from her chair. 'That is cruel, Father! I must not put aside the memory of my dear husband.'

'And you will weep for him forever?' he taxed. 'Comes a time when weeping must cease, being all exhausted. Will its cessation diminish the sense of loss any less then, or do we weep more for our own selves than for those who go to the arms of the Almighty? Would we then deprive them of that final celestial joy so hard earned in this world and wish them back into this one of strife and exactitude? Now is the time, Biddy, my dear, to look to your future and cease your weeping.'

She'd moved away from him as he spoke. Now she turned. 'You loved him too. How can you cast aside a true and loyal friend in such a way?'

'I do not cast him aside, Biddy. But I am allowed no time to weep. I have the settlement of a nation upon my shoulders and I must not weep for the past even though I long to. Thus does God mingle out the cup unto each of us and takes a friend and gives a friend.'

Bridget saw his eyes glimmer with tears and without his needing to say more, she saw the true depth of his loss of a beloved son-in-law who had been his greatest friend and companion from the time they had begun their strife against a king. In the face of such sadness she lowered her head and remained silent.

'And so,' came her father's voice with a sudden renewal of strength, rough with resolve to control his emotions. 'And so it remains that you appear to be attracted to Charles Fleetwood, else you would have turned him away before now. Do I think correctly?'

'You do, Father,' she allowed.

'And you would marry him should he ask?'

'I must have time.'

'Of course. But I will impart to you here and now what is in my mind. It's my desire to cause Colonel Charles Fleetwood to be Commander-in-Chief of Ireland. Were you to be his wife, you would again reign in Ireland rather than, shall we say, *others*?'

The connotation made her look up at him. His eyes were gleaming and she knew that he had already negotiated with Charles Fleetwood on a marriage. In this way was he meting out justice to those who'd insulted her, the wheels of his requital turning so quietly as to be hardly noticed by those who had offended.

Another might have deduced that he was using her for his own ends, but she knew different. He was doing this for her. Had she not shown affection towards Charles Fleetwood he would not have pressed it nor resorted to such measures. Gratitude filled her long-empty heart. Charles would continue to call on her with her father's blessing.

In her room, uninformed and so missing the point of it, Frances seethed with indignation and fury. How dare Papa turn away the one to whom her heart constantly flew, yet not six months after Bridget had been widowed shower his blessings upon her straying glance. So now she'd seek out Jerry White if possible, even though it would have to be done with cunning. The thought made her shiver with delicious joy for the danger it would involve.

'Parliament is to abolish the Lord Lieutenantship,' Oliver announced with great satisfaction at supper one midsummer evening, daylight still lingering to lift the spirits of his family.

In fine fettle, he had been playfully tormenting Frances by pushing pieces of chicory, the smell of which she hated, under her nose, chuckling when Mama ordered him to cease.

'This quarrel with the Netherlands is costing the country much,' he continued, everyone's attention now riveted by his statement. 'We'll make economies wherever possible. Abolition of the Lord Lieutenantship will help somewhat to reduce that debt.' He had generously returned his annual five thousand pounds on relinquishing that office to become Lord General.

Elizabeth was regarding him with a knowing light in her eye. 'Was not that post being offered to the Lamberts?'

He returned his wife's regard. 'A pity of course. But we must consider the nation's debt before all else. John Lambert has been offered the post of Commander-in-Chief in Ireland, unfortunately a lesser one than he had anticipated. We shall wait to hear whether or not he accepts it.'

'And what if he does not?' Mary burst out impulsively. But instead of looking askance at her, he gave her a benign smile.

'He will have to accept, little one, that being the only office now open to him. We shall see,' he added, muttering something concerning chess and gambit.

If he noticed the expression on Bridget's face, he ignored it, but it did not escape Frances, she innocently assuming her sister still to be labouring under her past grief despite being virtually affianced to Colonel Fleetwood. It was only later she learned that the post her father had referred to had already been offered to him. Nor was she aware that her father in his private game of chess was playing his best piece.

He played it well. Before long, news filtered through that Colonel Lambert had shown himself deeply insulted, in fact outraged by the offer he had been given. He'd apparently gone to enormous expense in readiness for becoming Lord Lieutenant of Ireland: a completely new wardrobe of clothing for himself and his wife, all of the finest quality; new furniture, silver plate and fine drapery; the best coach that money could buy, bloodstock horses of far superior quality than could be purchased in Ireland. Now it was all wasted, his pride preventing him from accepting the lesser post, as Oliver knew it would. Lambert was in check!

It was then that Oliver offered the position of Commander-in-Chief to Fleetwood, now Bridget's new husband, who readily accepted the offer that Lambert had spurned.

'Checkmate!' murmured Cromwell under his breath.

Nine

The dull season of Christmas dragged for Frances, with Mr White remaining at Hampton Court. Papa had decided to spend time with Betty, Bridget being in Ireland and Doll, having miscarried at seven months, too unwell to travel.

Even though Christmas was no longer the festive season, at least Betty's home was cheerful. Her candles and rushlights seemed to burn brighter and her windows to let in more light, the fine drapes at her tall elegant windows giving a sunny aspect.

Betty's preference was for pale tints – sky blue, apricot, turquoise, primrose, coral, rose pink – all picked out or bordered by gold. The rooms, lined with painted plaster rather than oak panels, escaped being dark and sombre and gave the house a sense of spaciousness even though it was not large, and each window gave out on to views of fen country with low horizons and a wealth of sky. It had been snowing and the wide sweep of untrodden whiteness looked like velvet and the weight of an overnight fall had made bare branches droop like willow trees.

Outside all was hushed and tranquil, but inside all was bright and busy, well worth the harrowing journey here even though Papa's private coach had taken the rutted roads and slithery wet snow well. Most of the time they had gone at a walk for fear the horses might break a leg, stranding them in the midst of nowhere.

A particularly heavy blizzard the first day had forced them to take shelter for the night at a dingy little village in an even dingier little inn. The food had been quite awful even though the landlord, overwhelmed at finding himself accommodating the Lord General himself, did what he could with his limited means.

His best room cleaned for them, he'd hovered and fussed, bowed and touched his forehead enough times to have given himself a headache, all the time rubbing his hands at his good fortune, for Papa had paid him well. Leaving next morning brought a crowd of villagers to see them off, the word rapidly passed round beforehand.

But for all the innkeeper's efforts, he'd not quite got rid of some less honoured guests, which Frances very soon discovered as pink itchy spots appeared on her upper arms and neck. Mary too began to squirm, though neither of their parents nor their brother Henry, who had come with them, complained at all.

'Our little sisters must have sweeter flesh,' he laughed. 'I daresay our tougher skins are better left untasted.'

It was good to gain Betty's home and have the itching allayed by some soothing ointment after everyone had been welcomed by her with hugs and kisses as well as warm handshakes from her husband John.

'You must be exhausted,' she flustered, her round, pretty face alive with joy as she ushered them into the blue-panelled drawing room where a most enormous log fire was blazing. 'But you are here now and a draught of hot spiced rum punch will soon warm you.'

'Would it not be wonderful to spend every Christmas here,' sighed Mary on their third day at Norborough. Lying full length on a Chinese rug before the crackling log fire in the drawing room, she watched a kitten from

Betty's extensive menagerie tying itself up in strands of embroidery thread. 'There's so much to do here. I could stay here forever.'

Frances said nothing. If only Jerry White could be with her, she too would have enjoyed staying here forever. The trysts they would arrange in the outhouses . . . the thought made her squirm deliciously. But Mr White was far away. Did he ever think of her as she thought of him at this moment? The looks he gave her when they did come within sight of each other told her that he must do.

'What a pity Henry is returning to Ireland soon,' Mary was saying. Tired of watching the kitten, she got up to stare out of the window at the deep snow that was keeping them here longer than expected. 'So nice having him here. I shall miss him. He's such a protective person and we are in such accord with each other. We are very close.'

He was Mary's favourite brother, but Frances had never felt close to him. Richard was her favourite. Against his brother's dependability, Dick seemed to her a vulnerable person that brought out a protective love from her. Dick was the older brother by fifteen months yet he often appeared the younger. Henry, sturdy, handsome, with a thick mane of tawny hair and a firm mouth beneath a strong moustache, had steady grey eyes like his father – a born soldier, a leader of men. Dick, however, was slender, gentle, his compliant features betraying an easygoing nature, a country gentleman. Dick would never make a soldier and didn't intend to.

'I shall write to Henry all the time,' Mary was prattling on. 'I wonder if he will ever find himself a wife.' The kitten had jumped on the windowsill and was trying to stalk Mary's fingers as she wriggled them about for it to catch. 'He should be thinking about it, you know, Frankie.' She turned sharply as no response came from her sister. 'Frankie, are you listening?'

Frances looked up with a start. She'd been thinking about Mr White.

'Of course I am,' she returned, vaguely aware that Mary had been speaking of Henry. She picked up a piece of charcoal and a scrap of paper lying beside her on the rug and began sketching a rough outline of a man's head and shoulders. 'You were saying Henry might marry.'

'I said he *should* marry,' replied Mary, testily. 'You've not listened! He's twenty-five and *should* be married. Lord Wharton's daughter, Ann, would be an ideal wife. He is a great friend of Papa and I'm sure he'd look most kindly on such a match. I've only seen her once – a very comely girl, and I remember Henry couldn't keep his eyes from her.'

Frances gave a grunt to show she was still listening though she was more engrossed in drawing a relatively good likeness of a young chaplain with a fine moustache.

Mary winced as the kitten's needle claw caught her finger. Pushing the animal off the windowsill she reflectively sucked at the tiny droplet of blood. 'I swear he has lost his heart to her. If I sent her a note on his behalf, who can say what might come of it? If he should take up with her and wed, he might even remain in England and be a person of great importance.'

But Frances had again forgotten to listen. She was pleased with her portrait of Jeremiah White. Taking it up, she folded it carefully and slipped it into the bodice of her dress. When she got to bed she would secretly gaze at it by the glow from the bedroom fire grate and dream that he lay beside her.

Returning home found all the problems Oliver had left behind still unsolved with a few more added, waiting like beggars at his door. Politics, the heavy burden that had become his life.

The stringy handful of politicians who constituted the

Rump had still not recovered from the crippling sea defeat before Christmas at the hands of the Dutch Admiral van Tromp. Oliver's own reputation didn't suffer and he came top of the elections once again. But his one-time friend and now jealous adversary, Sir Henry Vane, Chairman of the Admiralty Committee, hadn't fared at all well and Parliamentary esteem was low.

'They've no idea what they are doing,' Oliver complained to his wife, she ever a salve for his political bruises, a quiet and humble counsellor. Sitting with her in the evenings as he smoked his pipe, waistcoat unbuttoned, in stockinged feet, he would unburden his heart to her.

'The Army Committee is becoming impatient,' he said as she sat opposite him repairing a small hole in his second-best pair of black worsted stockings. 'There's little love this past year between Parliament and the Army, who repeatedly say that Parliament has lost its backbone.'

He shifted his position, uncrossing one leg and crossing it over the other, his movement intended to keep her attention. 'The Committee has long been calling for re-election. The House needs cleaning out and starting again. But it continually shelves the decision to dissolve itself and in truth has become the rump people call it. I am sick of it!'

Elizabeth glanced up at him in surprise. 'Will you resign then?'

'Indeed I will not!' he returned so harshly that she quickly resumed her task.

'I am and shall ever be,' he went on fervently, 'loyal to the Commonwealth for which I fought long and hard to achieve. I will serve it to the end of my days or until I am no longer wanted.'

Again she looked up, this time more certain of herself. 'You will always be wanted by the country, my dear,' she said, but he went on as though she hadn't spoken.

'Yet I must labour to bring matters to some proper

conclusion to suit Parliament, the Army and the people. Every Member of the House is merely eager to swell its numbers by recruitment and continue sitting happily with no need for re-elections. It is wrong. The Army knows it and I know it. It would consist of cronies interested only in lining their own pockets and wallowing in their own power. Corruption! A suppurating abscess!'

'Indeed so,' she adjoined, her sewing now idle on her lap.

'Three months has it spent – every Wednesday discussing dissolution and hardly any progress made. It has no intention of progressing. What I fear is that the Army will lose patience, as I am beginning to, and take it upon itself to clear the House by force. Another civil war? Friend against friend? I dare not contemplate what that would again do to the country.'

'What will you do?' prompted Elizabeth and he sighed heavily, his pipe lying loose between his fingers.

'All I can do is prevail upon the House to consider its own critical position. It must be persuaded to discuss the Bill of New Representative. We must have an election or the country will tumble back into anarchy – a ripe opportunity for young Charles Stuart to take hold and the Commonwealth to die after all we have fought for. It must not happen!'

There was a sharp snap as the clay pipe-stem broke between his clenched fingers and he regarded the two pieces, a better humour returning as his heavy lips curled.

'Waste of a good pipe,' he murmured.

From the window seat of the drawing room, Frances regarded her sister with horrified awe. 'How could you, Mall?'

'I saw no harm in it,' said Mary fretfully as she paced the room. 'I only did it for Henry's sake.'

'But to write to Lord Wharton himself, and in such a vein. What were you thinking of? He is a stranger to you.'

'He is Papa's friend.'

'But not yours. He must have thought you quite impudent.'

Mary ceased pacing to glare at her. 'You too thought it a good idea at the time.'

'I never did!' Occupied by dreams of Mr White at the time of Mary's proposal to play matchmaker, she hardly recalled what Mary had said. 'I assumed you were merely entertaining an idea, not intending to carry it out.'

Her sister came to stand over her. 'When I asked if it was what I should do, you affirmed it was.'

'I might have murmured something,' conceded Frances, 'but my mind wasn't on the subject. I didn't dream you'd go to such lengths to bring together Henry and a lady he hardly knows. He hasn't even professed any admiration for her. Nor did I condone any such move on your part and will not confess to being a party to it. All I can do is to speak for you when Papa gets here.'

Mary's pretty face had begun to crease. Her generous lips quivered as tears welled up in her dark eyes. She began pacing the floor again. 'What am I going to do? I never intended to make Papa look stupid in front of a friend of such great esteem. At the time I thought it would please Henry. Do you think Papa will be terribly angry? He has so much on his mind these days.'

Frances wondered if the day would come when he didn't have much on his mind. 'Perhaps he'll not be too angry,' she said. 'Mama is the one who seems the worse put out.'

When their parents finally arrived, Papa's expression held a look of distraction rather than anger – probably more trouble at the House. He looked tired and his face had a grey tinge. Sinking down on one of the wooden, straight-backed armchairs, his eyes portraying a patient weariness that came from long hours of arguing on political matters, he looked at Mary and patted a footstool by his chair.

'Come and sit by me,' he said and as she did so, went on, 'What a pretty little to-do we have here, do we not?'

Miserably Mary nodded while Frances and their mother waited on his next words. But as he looked down at the dark head bowed under his gaze, his heavy lips took on a soft smile.

'And what have we here before us?' he queried. 'A child – you are still a child, Mall, for all your sixteen years – writing some impertinent letter to an eminent man of title suggesting his daughter look kindly with a view of marriage upon a lesser man's son?'

Mary looked up sharply, humility forgotten for a moment. Her dark eyes glittered with passion. 'You're not a lesser man, Papa! You are great and well loved. Your name is on all the country's lips!'

He gave a sudden loud laugh, fatigue put aside. 'I commend you for your loving loyalty, my little wench. I would that this country were of the same accord, though I fear it is not. I see now that in doing what you did there was no mischief in it but that you meant only good. But I think Henry has no affection for the lady nor she for him, so let that be an end to it.'

He patted her head absently. 'In truth I think Wharton took no umbrage but was concerned lest something he'd not been informed of was taking place and merely wished to verify that there was nothing in it. I shall send a note prevailing upon him to let this affair slide easily off. And now not one more word to be spoken about it.' His tone lively, he gazed at his wife. 'And save the labour of our little Mall's feelings in case she incurs the loss of a good friend indeed.'

By which Frances took to mean their brother, who had been put to some embarrassment by the affair.

Oliver rose with an effort, sighing noisily. 'And now I must go back to Westminster though I swear I feel in no mood to wrangle much longer with those self-seekers.'

Another bout of stomach pain that had dogged him since the Scottish campaign was making it difficult to attend the House, and at a most critical time too. The Rump had regained its confidence since Blake's sea victory over van Tromp after a disastrous defeat in November. Puffed up, it was again overlooking the Bill of Elections whenever Oliver was absent.

'Three Wednesdays – three valuable weeks lost,' he groaned as daily he dragged himself from bed when the worst of the pain had subsided.

But not wholly lost. He was holding meetings of his own in his own house, attended by many who also saw the Rump as utterly self-centred – Members such as Bulstrode Whitelock, a long-term friend of his and a clever political lawyer. There was Harrison, who had no love for the Rump, and Lambert, who still blamed it for his loss of the Lord Lieutenantship of Ireland and was eager to see it fall.

'Colonel John Lambert still has no idea that his humiliation was Papa's work and not theirs,' giggled Mary with something like conspiratorial glee as she watched the arrivals and departures.

'And nor do we,' warned Frances significantly.

She was not interested in political crises, but what this one did mean to her was that Papa, with little time or inclination to go to Hampton Court, must ask his chaplains to come to the Cockpit to give their sermons. She hadn't seen Jerry White for nearly six weeks and it had been hard to smother the heartache their enforced estrangement had brought. There was a chance of seeing him here, but the house was small with nowhere to hide away with him and there were always people about. To be discovered with him was the last thing she wanted.

She prayed that whatever the outcome of this present business it would be soon, allowing them to resume their Sunday trips to Hampton Court. She longed for those secret nooks that littered the palace where she and Jerry had met in the past. It had happened quite unexpectedly just after Christmas. As the family returned to its own quarters, she holding back looking for a glimpse of him, she had heard a whisper behind her.

'Don't turn round, my lady.' She was often addressed so by many. 'I only wish to tell you that I will be in the kitchen area a quarter of an hour from now.'

She'd felt her palms grow moist, her stomach churn, her breath come fast and shallow and, not giving herself time to think, she had nodded. She had found him there and he had drawn her into a shadowy niche some way from the kitchens, the passage itself dim. There he had pressed her to the wall, shielding her body with his own so that to any passing it might look like he was kissing a serving maid. He had pressed his lips to hers in a long, hungry kiss. Her first she had ever experienced, she'd not quite known how to respond but she had been aware of a strange sensation spreading through her body, indefinable yet wonderful. Despite the length of the kiss, it was over too soon, though all day she could feel that pressure on her lips, recalling the sensation that had gone with it and a need for more.

From then on, when the family went to Hampton Court, this was their routine – the kiss, the marvellous feeling, the joy, the pain of parting, and the longing for next time. It hadn't gone beyond that ecstatic touch though an inner voice told her there was more to come, that a kiss would change in time to something more. 'Please let that change happen,' she prayed. She could not know then what changes there would be.

It was around the middle of April 1653 when Oliver returned from Westminster after a Wednesday sitting, his heavy features wreathed in smiles.

'Things go well, my dear,' he told his wife, striding across the hall towards her. His arm about her, he led her towards the drawing room.

'Come, Joan,' he said, using his name for her when he was in good spirits. 'We'll take a little sherry sack before supper. Lettie – supper in half an hour,' he called over his shoulder and the girl hurried off to tell their cook that the master was home early.

In the drawing room Elizabeth poured sherry then sat across the hearth from him. The fire was low, for it wasn't a cold evening. Indeed April had been something of a warm month.

Appreciatively savouring the sherry, he put the half empty glass down to regard his wife. 'The Bill of Elections has finally been discussed in full. The final consideration will be next Wednesday and I am promised there will be no more laying aside. There'll be new representatives in the autumn. So we have it.' He leaned back in his chair. 'A new elected Parliament composed of good and saintly men.' Taking up his glass he drained the rest in one gulp. 'I'm well pleased. There'll be no more talk of any mixed monarchical government as was visualised eighteen months ago.'

'Ah, the settlement of the nation,' mused Elizabeth, remembering that protracted question of a mix of republic and monarchy when Mr Bulstrode Whitelock had asked what sort of settlement it was to be. There'd been debate over on whom such a power would fall and fears of it necessitating the recall of an obscure member of the Stuarts.

But Oliver had been more concerned when his own name had been put forward, and though he'd turned it away from himself the question had worried him.

Elizabeth was the last to wish the role of ruler on him. All her life she had led a simple existence. Greatness was not for her, nor would she ever seek it, not for her and not for Oliver, but there had long been this underlying hint that he might serve his country by taking a crown. She knew he never would, and for herself felt she could never have borne the illustrious and frightening title of queen.

Interpreting her expression, Oliver smiled disarmingly. 'It has been settled well enough, and no more fears, Joan, my dear.'

She was filled with relief. 'Then your conversation with Mr Whitelock in St James's Park on your possible kingship has resolved itself. I am so thankful.' She was alarmed to see Oliver's face darken.

'I did not speak to him on the subject of *my* kingship, but on the consequences arising should a man take it upon himself to be king. There is a deal of difference, Elizabeth.'

He having dropped the endearment of Joan, she felt herself blush and quickly lowered her head over her own glass. Instantly his temper melted.

'Joan, my dear! I did not mean to reproach you.' He leaned forward to take her smooth hand in his large capable one. 'Rather I wish to forget I ever strolled or spoke with Whitelock that day last November and I pray he does likewise. I cringe that I could have been so imprudent as to speak my dilemma aloud. Each time I see the man I feel out of countenance that he knows my deepest soul-searching and could make whatever he wished of it. I was troubled, but how I long for the words I said to that man to have been left unspoken, for they would damn me forever as a self-seeking man should he ever reveal them.'

'No, my dearest!' She was on her knees, burying her face in his hands as she wept with love for the humblest man she had ever known. 'Never will you be thought of as self-seeking!' And it took a while for him to lift her up, so filled with tears was she.

It was the nineteenth of April, the eve of the Commons' promised final discussion, and the Army was still ready with a vote of no confidence in the Rump. Lambert paced the upstairs room of the Cockpit where the meeting had been called, his voice raised.

'I've little trust in any of you,' he shouted at those who were there. 'Whatever provisions are made in regard to the electorate, who is to say you will not find some way to control it to your own advantage?'

Murmurs of doubt followed his accusations while the Rump Members did their best to persuade the officers of the integrity of their promises, while safely out of the way downstairs the women of the Cromwell household bit their lips at the raised voices going on well into the night.

'Why do they argue so?' Mary asked her mother, who shook her head.

'It is the officers who question. Your father told me that he obtained the Commons' promises, so this dissention must be of the Army's doing. That is the way of men, to shout and bluster. It will come out settled in the end.'

But when the meeting finally broke up there was still no truce.

'I say this,' Oliver was heard to say as everyone departed. 'Power must pass out of the hands of this present government and into the hands of those who will make better use of it. I promise you that six men will do the Lord's work better in one day than this Parliament has done in a hundred!'

'How did it go?' ventured Elizabeth when he finally

came down to share a few moments with her before retiring to bed.

'A rough passage,' he told her, rubbing at his eyelids with finger and thumb. 'But I have assurance that they will try to suspend proceedings about the bill for a representative until they have a further conference.'

'Are you satisfied with that?' she asked, surprised after the hubbub.

'I am.' He dropped his hand and smiled at her, looking tired and strained. 'And have agreed. I look forward to tomorrow's debate, when some such issue will give satisfaction to all.'

With this he rose, grunting with the effort like a man twice his age. 'And now to bed,' he sighed, putting an affectionate arm about her as she too rose, and guided her from the room.

Ten

1653

Cromwell had been assured nothing would happen in the Commons until the afternoon, so the meeting with his officers at his home was leisurely.

Even his dress was casual, reflecting his relaxed attitude. Shoes well worn and pliable, grey worsted stockings – a darn on one calf quite visible – black breeches shiny from sitting, a plain black coat with rubbed elbows and a collar that looked to have seen many wearings since it last saw a washtub.

'As you see,' he laughed, 'I am at ease in my own home. So smirk you all!' And he wagged a playful finger at them. 'I care not a fig for the convention of your own modishness. But after discussion and a good luncheon I'll attire myself better and we will off to Westminster to hear the Commons' debate. And so to our business then.'

At ease they settled down with no urgency to discuss an interim council. By eleven o'clock their light mood matched the April sunshine streaming through the square-paned windows of the upstairs room. Ale was brought, quaffed generously. Thoughts of the appetising luncheon for which Lady Cromwell was becoming known caused stomachs to rumble. No one took much note of the thumping upon the street door until Oliver's house manager, Maidstone, knocked on the room door, to be thrust aside by a breathless messenger.

'My lords! The House is packed. Upon my oath, Lord Cromwell, every Member must be there. The Bill is to be discussed immediately.'

His eyes roamed over those in the room, returning again to Cromwell. 'I came straight away, sir. It wouldn't have been fair to have not come.'

For a while Cromwell stared back, his smile fixed like a grimace on a stone gargoyle. Then, as if struck by a whip, movement returned. In a matter of seconds he was calling for messengers to be sent to the House to see what exactly was happening. Ten minutes later came the clatter of booted feet on the stairs and as one the assembly stood up to receive a distraught Colonel Ingoldsby.

'Cromwell! How can I say? An Act is being discussed even as I speak. It is occasioning other meetings of the Members to prolong their own existence. Nothing of the Bill of New Representative, only the prolongation of this present Parliament. And you and your Members not there . . .'

More pounding up the stairs cut him short and another messenger burst in.

'Sirs – the Act is almost through!'

Again Cromwell came to life in a burst of fury, took hold of the chair where he had so recently been sitting at ease and flung it down. His voice thundered across the room.

'God be my witness! I did not believe such persons could do it!'

Minutes later, a party of musketeers of his regiment with him, he'd dashed from his house, through Whitehall, to burst into an astonished House of Commons.

The chamber was indeed packed, but from the hush that fell at his entrance, it might easily have been deserted. Every eye turned as he stood, his face flushed, his breathing laboured and quite audible in the stillness. Unbecoming at the best of times, notorious for his disinterest in clothes, today it was as if a madman had burst in.

Recovering himself, he bowed formally to Mr Speaker William Lenthall, who in turn collected his composure enough to acknowledge him, then went to his place in the chamber.

His soldiers left outside, he sat without moving, one elbow supported by the bench behind him, and gnawed at a thumbnail. For a few minutes he listened then got slowly to his feet. Once more all eyes turned towards him as he began to speak, his voice calm though all instinctively felt that beneath this calm a lion crouched ready to spring.

They were correct in that thinking. Soon he was pacing the chamber, his toneless voice rising, his words growing more impassioned.

'You think to extend your miserable existence in this House, safe as worms in rafters eating away till the roof falls ruinous about your heads. No, I say, no! Not while I can remedy such desecration of a nation's well-being. This marvellous Commonwealth was gotten with the blood of good men, built on the bones of our saintly dead. And you, sirs, will bring all that to naught with your seeking after power. You are, all of you, suckers of blood. Worse, you are corrupt to your very souls.'

He began picking out individuals as he paced, an arm held straight out, accusing finger pointing directly at this one and that. 'You are a glutton, sir. You, a lover of soft living. And you, a drunkard! You, a whoremonger! And you, sir, are a scandal to the profession of the Gospel!'

Each Member thus singled out leapt to his feet appealing to Speaker Lenthall. Soon the chamber was in uproar, hats being frantically waved, fists lifted in righteous anger, cloaks flapping. Amid all this, the resonant voice of the Speaker calling for order was but the squeak of a mouse, yet above it all an impassioned Cromwell could still be heard.

'You think this not Parliamentary language. I confess it is not. Neither are you to expect any from me.'

Sir Peter Wentworth, grandson of an eminent Parliamentary leader during the old Queen Elizabeth's reign, leapt to the floor of the chamber to confront Cromwell face to face.

'Sir, cease this abuse at once! We do not expect this from one so highly trusted.'

'Come!' was the shouted reply. 'I will put an end to your prating. You are no Parliament. I say you are no Parliament! I will put an end to your sitting.' Turning from Wentworth, he signalled to Colonel Harrison. 'Call them in!'

In seconds some thirty armed musketeers were inside the chamber. As Harrison came to him, Oliver pointed to Speaker Lenthall perched on his chair. 'Fetch him down.'

'But Lord Cromwell,' protested Harrison, 'the work is great and dangerous. It should not be done.'

'Fetch him down, I say, or I will.' The blazing grey eyes fixed on him and Harrison's feeble protest melted. Grabbing the Speaker's gown he dragged him from his seat.

'Empty the House!' bellowed Cromwell amid cries of outrage.

'This is not honest,' yelled Henry Vane from the other side of the chamber. 'This is against morality and common honesty.'

Oliver's reaction was immediate, his voice taunting. 'Oh, Sir Henry Vane, Sir Henry Vane, the Lord deliver us from Sir Henry Vane!'

With that he grabbed up the mace lying before the Speaker's chair.

'Here!' He thrust the heavy object into the hands of a musketeer. 'Take this fool's bauble away.'

'And you are but a juggler!' Vane yelled at him as with dozens of others he was bundled from the chamber by soldiers.

'It is you,' Oliver yelled after him, 'who have forced me

to do this, for I've sought the Lord day and night that he rather slay me than put me to do this work.'

As the House cleared he snatched up the parchment containing the Act of Dissolution lying discarded and unpassed by the ejected Parliament before following them out, leaving a silent and empty House behind him.

'Have you heard?' laughed Frances. 'Someone has fixed a sign outside the House of Commons: "This house to let, now unfurnished."'

'It is no laughing matter.' Her mother's sharp reprimand sobered her. 'Your father took no pleasure in his work and has sought the Lord ever since the doing of it. So do not mock, young lady.'

'It was cleverly put, though,' Frances said later to Mary.

But Mary did not seem disposed to side with her. 'Some say Papa was wrong to do what he did and only Parliament can dissolve itself.'

They were sitting on low stools brought out to the garden for the warm May sunshine. The lawns were full of daisies and Frances was making a little chain of them to tie in her hair. Angrily she let them fall. 'Is that what you think?'

'Not what I think but what is being said.'

Mollified a little, Frances gazed down at the fallen, pink-edged flowers. 'Whether it's true or not, Papa is being lauded throughout the land for his action. It's said the Rump was riddled with corruption and even the Speaker is being called to account over some suspicious profits he has made out of his office.'

Her sister didn't reply but gazed up at the tiny white clouds floating in a depth of blue. With her silence transmitting itself to her as disapproval, Frances hurried on with her defence of their father, the love for whom seemed strangely not so strong in Mary these days. Perhaps Mary was growing away from childish adoration, being sixteen now and a woman. But Frances too was coming up to womanhood, being only six months from her fifteenth birthday, yet she hadn't lost her love for Papa.

'They say Parliament deliberately introduced a New Recruiter clause into the Act of Dissolution so as to control the elections in November. Papa was quite justified in doing what he did and I can't see why you are not of the same opinion, Mall.'

'I am of the same opinion,' she said sharply. 'But Mama said that he was so infuriated that he cast the Act of Dissolution into the fire and now no one will ever know what it contained so who will ever be able to say whether he was right or wrong in what he did?'

Still a little angry, Frances got up and wandered off but turned to look back at her sister. 'Whatever it held, people had long ago lost all respect for that Parliament. Everyone suspected it to be out for its own ends, and Papa is being spoken of as a champion. They sing his praises even in Europe. Our house is filled with foreign diplomats and ambassadors looking on him as a new ruler. Preachers here in London are saying he is deserving of a crown.'

At this a spark of harmony gleamed in Mary's eyes. 'So I've heard.'

Coming to join Frances, she linked arms and for a while they stood in silence gazing at the formal garden of their home with its neat beds of blue and cream heartsease, deep rose love-lies-bleeding and scented herbs, all bordered by tiny box hedges and grassy walks. The fruit trees were in bloom and a stone bird bath stood on a little plinth, while further on there was a brick dovecot full of white and grey flutterings in a haste to feed the squabs that would be ready for the table next winter.

'Do you think he should take the crown were it offered? Mary asked.

'I don't know,' replied Frances.

'Do you think it will be offered?'

'I cannot say. Do you think it will?'

Mary shrugged. 'If he did become king, we'd be princesses. We could do anything we wanted. We could choose to marry whomever we like and you could marry your Jeremiah White.'

'That's silly!' Frances pulled away from Mary's arm. 'As princesses we'd have even less choice. We'd be made to marry some prince from some other country. That's how it's done.' Visions of not seeing Jerry again made her feel ill. 'I hope Papa never takes a crown. I shall pray to God he never does. I love Jerry White so. If I could never have him, I think I should die.'

Mary stared at her as tears filled her eyes. 'I didn't think of that,' she said slowly and took her arm again to offer comfort. 'I shall pray he doesn't, then maybe all will return to normal and we shall be as we always were.'

With eyes downcast, Frances nodded, surveying the fallen daisies that had so lately been a sweet chain in her hands, now scattered on the grass to wilt and die.

To the delight of Frances some return to normal came when at the end of May Sunday visits to Hampton Court were resumed. But a certain grandeur had crept into the occasion. Simple as was their worship of God, other things had become not as simple, a ceremony creeping into everything. A glittering troupe of outriders now accompanied them to Hampton Court. Father's coach bore a fluttering standard with the colours of his regiment. Men would doff their hats and women would curtsy as their coach passed. At Hampton Court crowds gathered to watch them arrive and depart.

Mary had forgotten her promise to pray that all would return to normal, her eyes bright at her family's increasing importance. But Frances felt her heart grow heavy at the pressure that importance would have on her when the time came for Papa to introduce her to a suitor.

Marriage was indeed on her family's mind at this moment but in the shape of Henry, much to Mary's joy, having been bitterly put out when not long after her disastrous attempt at matchmaking he began pursuing a certain Dorothy Osborne.

'A Royalist!' snorted Mary in disgust. 'And such a puffed-up young woman. I shouldn't think Papa will approve.'

'There is little he can do,' remarked Frances. 'Henry is a man and whether Papa approves or not he will have his own way, whereas his daughters must submit to his choosing of husbands for them.'

Her bitter remark going unnoticed, Mary said, 'We will marry into fine families and be glad of Papa's choice when we are great and well respected. But for Henry to cast his eye upon the daughter of a Royalist will not please Papa. What is he thinking of?'

Henry's path to true love in Dorothy Osborne's direction, however, had not been smooth. He'd written to Bridget's husband in Ireland to procure a fine greyhound for him to present to his love, knowing her passion for that breed, but before it was delivered he found that she had a secret lover, a William Temple.

'Poor Henry,' sighed Mary, who had a wonderful gift for knowing the smallest scandal before it had become generally bandied about. 'She was even using Henry to taunt the man – to make him jealous, I imagine.'

'Where did you hear all this?' Frances taxed her.

'From Betty – she knows all the London gossip. I'm glad she is staying with us again for a while. Life is so jolly when she is here. But poor Henry – how will he ever get over it?'

But Henry had already caught sight of Elizabeth Russell, daughter of a good Parliamentarian and old colleague of Papa, Sir Francis Russell of Chippenham. As well as being extremely pretty, she was far more exemplary in her ways than the wayward Dorothy Osborne, and within a week both fathers had given Henry's proposal of marriage their blessing.

'It may be,' said Frances with a mind on Jerry White after a splendid wedding at Whitehall, 'that now Papa's problems of state are over, he'll feel more disposed to look kindly on his youngest daughter's affections of the heart.'

This hope she clung to as she and Jerry continued to keep their secret trysts in the shadowy niches of the dim kitchen corridor with its stone flags to warn them of any but a servant's approach – being easily discernable by a hurrying step rather than one of calmer purpose – though none but servants came here.

There were times when she had an unsettling feeling that Papa might be having her watched, but if he were, there was certainly no intimation of it and he treated her as lovingly as ever. She was almost persuaded at times to reveal her feelings for Jerry and throw herself on Papa's loving indulgence, for she hated the intrigue. But some vague sense of foreboding always stopped her. Were Papa to forbid it, how could she go against him? So long as he remained in ignorance she could continue with at least some easiness of mind.

Yet was he entirely unaware? His very greatness had come from being well informed of all that went on. There wasn't much that missed him. Was he content to humour her until her apparent infatuation burned itself out or was he allowing his chaplain enough rope to hang himself? He'd done such to others – men he'd called friend. She remembered Colonel Lambert, he still with no knowledge who had engineered his loss of Lord Lieutenantship of

Ireland and who saw her father as a friend. A quiet, unobtrusive quittance that had been done with patience and stealth. Papa could be a frighteningly patient man when he wished, and it was this she feared.

But love made her reckless. It was recklessness that took her on this Sunday morning in June to their gloomy meeting place, her heart beating as always with sickening thumps of excitement.

Sitting with the congregation listening to the sermon from a preacher on his tall pulpit, she'd seen Jerry in the shadow of a doorway, his eyes on her. As their glances met he made a small gesture with his head and slipped back into the darkness behind him. Knowing full well what that gesture meant, when the sermon was over and the congregation began to disperse she'd slipped away towards the kitchens, the hood of her light cloak hiding her face.

Now in the recess he kissed her, passionately, making her gasp for joy. His hands on her breast trembled. His voice came hoarsely. 'We cannot continue this way. We must meet elsewhere, somewhere more private, and for a longer time. I need you . . .'

'I cannot,' she sighed. 'Not for longer. We should be discovered.' Yet she too dearly wanted more than these few snatched moments.

'There is a corridor little used at this time of day,' he was saying as though she had never protested. 'It lies above and just beyond the King's Chamber and leads to the servants' quarters. Go there quickly.'

'But luncheon will be—'

'Quickly!'

He broke off as footsteps came along the stone corridor, hurrying in the way servants do. Jerry stepped out from the alcove and hurried off, leaving her bewildered as to what to do. The youth that passed her – hardly more than a boy, in a leather apron and holding some iron tool or other – glanced at her as he passed. Recognising a daughter of the great Lord General Cromwell, he dipped his moving body in an awkward bow, lifting the iron tool incongruously to his forelock, and mumbled an embarrassed and surprised 'm'lady' and went on his way.

Just a little less startled and now alarmed, Frances peeped in the direction Jerry had taken, but he was gone. The kitchen boy must have seen them together. Would he make anything of it? Perhaps he was too simple to do so. But it only needed him to tittle-tattle.

She should go straight back upstairs to the great hall where the usual drove of Sunday guests gathered for their meal, but she had to warn Jerry, ask him what best to do now.

Hurrying up a flight of narrow wooden stairs, along one silent corridor after another – much of it familiar, she and Mall having explored them all in the past – until finally she came to one that led behind the King's Chamber, seldom used by anyone, Papa having no stomach for anything kingly.

The corridor was deserted, silent – not even a distant murmur of voices – and terminated in a narrow wooden stairway, very worn and neglected. At the far end was a single window, the only source of light. Along its length were three doors. She recognised this as an area often called the haunted gallery, and indeed it seemed to hold an echo all its own. Frances shivered.

The opening of a door beside her without warning almost snatched the life from her body. As she let out a little cry, a voice came from the darkened aperture.

'In here! Quickly!'

Her heart thumping from the fright, although she now knew it had been Jerry's voice, she went in and he closed the door quietly. The merest chink of sunlight pierced drawn drapes to reveal an empty room but for the odd piece of furniture to be put out of the way.

'I thought you might not come.' His voice was low, and when she made no reply he took her gently by the shoulders, turning her to face him.

In the dimness his handsome features glowed pale as he brought her closer and all fear drained from her as she let herself be folded in his arms. Feeling wonderfully limp she sought his comfort and support and forgot all about the warning she'd meant to convey to him.

At first his lips touched hers lightly, such a delightful sensation, then as they pressed harder her body seemed to leap inside her as though it were a single living flame and she heard her own stifled voice whimpering with pleasure and a need she could not define – the same undefined need she always felt when kissed by him, but this time far more urgent. She only knew that she wanted the sensation to last forever.

She felt him lift her, carry her to the centre of the room and set her down on a coverlet spread on the boards. Oddly enough she could not have stood unaided, for her knees and legs seemed incapable of supporting her.

'Frances, my dear heart.' His voice held a strangled note. 'I have so long yearned for you.'

He was lying over her, his body light, his kisses covering her face, and the spicy masculine scent of his skin filled her nostrils, exciting her into clutching him to her. This was far more wonderful than standing in a cold dark alcove.

There was an intimate firmness of purpose to his hand as it roamed her body to force a trembling sigh from her. She became aware of the hand moving to seek the secret place beneath her skirts and as some primitive instinct of self-preservation took hold, she tensed. Immediately his hand became still and he lifted himself slightly from her.

'I would not hurt you, my love,' he whispered. 'You are all to me – my very life. I would not harm you.'

As she lay limp beneath him, already some unknown thing told her this was what happened between man and woman, that if she wanted to still this strange craving that was beginning to consume her and drive her mad, she must let it happen, whatever it was.

He seemed to divine her thoughts, for he lowered himself against her and once more the hand moved, this time without impediment. Oh, the sensation of its movements inside her! Gone the fear, in its place a need like a great heat inside her. She was hardly aware of his entry until a sharp stab of agony made her cry out.

'Oh, please, it hurts!' But he didn't stop, merely gasped, 'It will go, my love. It'll go.' And gritting her teeth she felt the stab give way to a sweeter sensation, again almost unbearable enough to have her gasping with the strange glory of it, yet not painful.

Suddenly it was over. Grunting from his exertions, he eased himself from her to lie inert while she lay staring up at the dingy ceiling, clarity now returning and with it shame as without warning she burst into tears, causing him to sit up.

'Please don't be upset,' he comforted. 'I'd never harm you. I am in love with you and I intend to marry you. I shall approach your father this very day and beg for your hand in marriage.'

'He will not consent,' she sobbed. 'It's not only that – it was sinful what we did. He must never know. I can't bear it.'

Hardly knowing what she was doing, she was on her feet, her legs feeling weak as she adjusted her skirts. Running from the room she knew he hadn't followed, but was unsure whether he should have or not as she ran back the way she'd come to let herself out through a door to the gardens beyond.

A servant sent to find her discovered her in a rose arbour. Her excuse for the reddened eyes was a fearful headache that had caused such a feeling of nausea that she had sought the open air, unable to look at food much less partake of it. It was a worried father who ordered her to bed to recover rather than request her to join her family and their friends.

Eleven

Betty was allowing Henry's new wife her sympathetic understanding.

'I'm sure they couldn't have meant to be so hurtful. It does seem the lot of any prominent family to be twitted and lampooned. I'm sure it was done light-heartedly.'

The day wet and dreary despite it being the height of summer, the five young Cromwell women sat in Mary's room, a preferred place to chat and exchange confidences away from the ears of servants and the intrusion of menfolk.

Betty and Dorothy had stayed on at the Cockpit since Henry's marriage, Betty's husband's work keeping him in London, often in the company of a Mr Christopher Wren, a young architect – he with lists of calculations and Mr Wren with sheaves of drawings – and Doll because she was pregnant again.

Richard thought it best for her not to return home until the baby was well established inside her. In her delicate third month, the trauma of coach travel – albeit in their own comfortable private coach – might prove too much for her. In fact it could be plainly seen how thin and wan she was. The loss of her second child and a following miscarriage had drained her.

At the moment it was Henry's wife who was down in the mouth for all Betty's efforts to cheer her. The reason for it was persistent calling out after her and Henry when taking the air in the public Spring Gardens.

It had begun with some wit crying out, 'Way for the Prince!' which had brought titters from other strollers familiar with the rumour – and it was only a rumour – that Lord General Cromwell, with an eye to the crown, had ordered one to be privately made for him, and the taunt 'Way for the Prince!' had virtually become a by-word.

'It's come to such a pitch,' young Elizabeth sighed, 'that Henry and I no longer dare walk abroad.'

'You aren't the only ones to suffer public banter,' said Mary. 'Mama also complains of it. That's why Papa is thinking of closing the Gardens.'

'Who can blame him?' Dorothy gazed lovingly down at her three-year-old daughter, Beth, playing at her feet with a cloth doll. Beth was her father-in-law's favourite granddaughter. 'I would blush to be called after. This family is no longer respected.'

'It's greatly respected,' protested Mary. 'There'll always be fools who lampoon that which they themselves cannot attain. For what point is there in ridiculing the lowly and commonplace? Our greatness alone promotes such reactions, but we shall weather it.'

'Papa certainly does,' remarked Frances, unable to keep the acidity out of her tone.

She stood leaning on the window seat to gaze down into the street at a group of urchins throwing mud at each other. A woman shouted at them as a bit caught her skirt, leaving several young girls to giggle into their aprons at the scene. Two men passing had wide-brimmed hats pulled low against the rainy afternoon so that with faces hidden none could know what they were thinking. They reminded her of Papa. These days she couldn't tell what he was thinking either, except that sometimes he would gaze at her, whether in displeasure or contemplation it was hard to say. Only yesterday she had enquired if anything was amiss and he'd countered by asking if she thought there should be, to which she had no reply.

'It's as though Papa was above it all and already a royal personage.' She turned as they gasped and saw them looking at her in shocked surprise. 'Do you not recall,' she enlightened, 'just a fortnight ago when we were with him in St James's Park and someone passing neglected to raise his hat to Papa?'

'I wasn't there,' Betty said.

'But you were, Mall – you and Mama. It was always customary for a man to raise his hat to the monarch on meeting. It has now become accepted that the same mark of respect is due to Papa as the acknowledged head of the country. But I felt quite discomforted by the incident.'

'What happened?' asked Elizabeth, her pretty mouth agape.

The man made to pass as if Papa were of no consequence. But Papa stepped in front of him and said, as if in sociable jest, that when the Duke of Buckingham failed to doff his cap to the late King he'd had it knocked off for him by another, and that he too could be in similar peril, and not even a duke to the bargain. I've never seen anyone doff his hat so quickly or go so red in the face. And I've never felt so truly conspicuous.'

'I felt not the least conspicuous,' put in Mary. 'Isn't respect what is due to us as the First Family in the land?'

And will Papa be king, thought Frances, and we princesses? But she kept the thought to herself, turning back to the window and leaving the others to their gossip. Would she be obliged to marry a lord or a duke or even a prince and say farewell to her true love?

The Lord General was working on some papers in his

Whitehall office when Jeremiah White begged audience with him.

He found his patron seated in a high-backed, ornately carved chair behind a wide, leather-covered oak table. But instead of continuing to study his papers and leaving his visitor to wait upon his pleasure, he immediately rose to his feet.

'Doctor White, a while since I saw you last,' he beamed, affably using the new title for his chaplain for his having done good study of theology.

Everything about Cromwell was amiable, the outstretched hand indicating a nearby chair, the florid face wreathed in a smile about the robust nose that caused his enemies to delight in calling him Old Ruby Nose – a thought Jeremiah hastily put from him as he took the offered seat.

'That's it,' urged Cromwell. 'We do not stand on ceremony.'

As Jeremiah sat, Cromwell settled himself back into his own chair, fingers loosely linked, forefingers caressing his lower lip as he studied his visitor. 'Now, what brings me the pleasure of your company?'

Jerry squirmed and gnawed at the inside of his cheek. 'Sir, may I first take this opportunity to thank you again for all you have done for me? I shall ever be in your debt.'

The grey eyes twinkled. 'I have a high regard for you, my boy, and did consider you worth sending to Oxford. But you haven't come here merely to thank me for what I would do for any man that showed a grain of eagerness to pursue the enviable profession of preaching the Lord's word. No, I see more in your visit. If you are troubled or in need of advice, how can I be of service to you? As you see, I am here to be of help to any that wants it.'

Had he not been so concerned by the need of his errand, Jerry might have smiled at this long-windedness, Cromwell known as a man incapable of making the simplest statement without turning it into a speech.

He wasn't here to listen to speeches. 'Sir, I *am* somewhat troubled,' he began cautiously, steeling himself. 'Sir, my problem concerns the Lady Frances – if I may be so bold as to refer to her by name before her loving parent.'

He waited for some response, a warning frown, a questioning look, but the benign face failed to betray anything. Taking heart he ploughed on.

'I confess I find your daughter as charming and sweet-natured as any could be. I have long been attracted to her – from afar. But some time back we chanced to speak together and I have to tell you, sir, that from that time a tender friendship has struck up between us. And for her part, sir, the Lady Frances does not seem averse to me.'

Still there was no reaction. Cromwell was like a carved image, his fingertips still against his lips, the lips smiling, but the smile was fixed, neither encouraging nor reproving, his very silence telling him he was expected to continue. Jerry ran a moistening tongue across his lower lip.

'I find it difficult to approach you on this subject, sir, and I entreat you to take no offence at my audacity. I would ask if you could look kindly on my friendship with your sweet daughter – my close friendship, my . . . my growing love for her – in time that I may come to you to . . . to ask for her hand . . .' He was talking himself to a standstill and he let his words trail off before that steady, disconcerting, steel-grey gaze that seemed to be locking his in an invisible grip.

The man stirred at last. The forefingers were lowered, the smile faded. Almost leisurely Cromwell got up to pace about, head bent, hands clasped behind his back, his steps measured. 'I pray you bear with me in what I must say,' he began. His tone low, he went on, 'I consider myself not an intolerant parent and am sympathetic to any God-fearing man's affection towards my most treasured daughter, but do ask you to consider her tender years, that December – which is yet four months away – will see her fifteenth year on this earth of ours.'

'I do consider it, sir,' Jerry dared to interrupt. 'And I am content to wait.'

'You are content to wait.' It was less a question than a condemnation as the Lord General regarded him with a penetrating stare. 'And how long are you prepared to wait, Doctor White? A year? Two years? Five? How strong are your affections for my daughter that they could sustain you five years or contain your natural desires?'

Remembering what had happened in that empty room, words to the effect that he was strong enough and constant enough wouldn't come, and he sat silent as Cromwell resumed his pacing.

'I have no dislike of you. Indeed I have a high regard for the zealous and virtuous principles I presume one of your office to hold. Thus you will appreciate the loving concern of any father for his child, his instinct to protect, to fend off any element that might cause her pain or anguish in her innocence of the harshness of this world. I would therefore ask, no, beg you to stand a moment in the place of a doting father and in that light understand and bear with his wish that his daughter be not harassed by a suitor of any sort until her father is of a loving opinion that the time is ripe for her to meet the occasion as a grown woman. As a righteous and godly-minded man I am sure you do understand what I am saying and will humour this loving parent's wishes until he feels his daughter is old enough.'

With this he turned suddenly to fix his visitor with a friendly but discriminating gaze and, taken off guard, Jerry could only nod agreement.

Moments later he was outside in the corridor, the Lord General's door closed on him after a friendly slap on the shoulder and a 'God's day to you' as an amiable but positive dismissal and with little idea as to how his audience with this man had come to be terminated so swiftly. Worse, he had been left not only feeling more like a chastened schoolboy than a respected minister, but also with an uncomfortable conviction that the man was more aware of what was going on between him and Frances than he'd imagined.

There was a new face at the Cockpit – a William Dutton, a young man with an angelic face and impeccable manners – though one more face made little difference in this house of constant comings and goings.

'I wonder Mama stands it,' remarked Mary as she and Frances sat with knees drawn up under their skirts on the lawn of their garden on a warm and sunny October afternoon. 'I've never known a house so constantly full of people. Even Betty and John have to put up with one tiny room at the back of the house. She is there now, lying down.'

'I did hear she was poorly this morning,' said Frances absently, her mind on other things.

It was Friday. Tomorrow morning they'd be off to Hampton Court, Papa taking in as much time as he could before winter made travel impossible. They'd be going by river, more pleasant than by road. They'd have gone more often by water but that Papa felt they should at times be seen by the people.

She wondered what reception she would get from Jerry. These last two weeks she was certain he'd been avoiding her. Was he, like she, fearful of repeating what had happened in that empty room, even regretting it, wishing it had never happened. She could still feel the shame of it as much as her heart went over and over at the thought of him.

'Doctor Goddard has seen her.' Mary brought her

thoughts back to the present. 'He's diagnosed a colic and she is to take only milk and bland food. Did you know' – she turned to Frances with her newest snippet of news – 'she's had this same pain almost a year? She masks it so well and is so lively, none had any idea she suffered so. It must be exceptionally bad for her to spend such a lovely afternoon in bed.'

Mary moved her position on the grass, autumn dampness penetrating her skirts. 'I hope she recovers quickly. When she's here we see more life in one week than ever we do in a year without her. She is on the closest terms with people like the Lamberts and speaks of them as John and Frances, and Countess Dysart she calls Bess, quite as if they'd been friends from childhood.'

'Papa too calls her Bess,' Frances pointed out. It seemed to her he referred to the frivolous Countess Dysart a little too readily by her given name. 'I don't think Mama approves – far too intimate for someone of his standing.'

Mary wasn't listening. 'Betty and John really should have a better room than they have. But there is simply no room anywhere. I can't see why Papa allows so many people to stay. Papa's mother is here, and there is the whole family of his old valet, Jean Duret, who died while nursing Papa back to health. I know Dick and Doll have returned home but now comes this William Dutton. Papa is going to pay for his tutoring, I hear.'

Mention of their newest guest made Frances frown. Why should Papa take in a young man whose father, Sir Ralph Dutton, had been a staunch Royalist, a gentleman of the privy chamber extraordinary to King Charles?

'What reason has he to make himself responsible for the son of a sworn Royalist?' she queried. 'Even if he is orphaned.'

Mary looked thoughtful. 'I know his father's brother came on to Parliament's side during the civil war and grew to become a firm colleague of Papa. He had been a Royalist but was imprisoned by the King for refusing to do something or other that he thought unfair and he went over to the Parliamentarians because of it.'

'That's no reason for Papa to bring his nephew here, unless he had a motive. He usually has.'

'Oh, come now, Frankie,' chided Mary. 'It's nice having a young man our own age under our roof. Don't you think he's handsome and charming?'

'I've not given it much thought. He's hardly been here long enough for me to have had time to notice.'

She chose to ignore her sister's disbelieving laugh. She had indeed studied Master Dutton, though she wasn't giving her sister that satisfaction. His arrival did not sit well with her. There *was* an ulterior motive – she was sure of it – and she felt angry that Papa should deem her so gullible as not to see through his ruse. She wasn't a silly child not to suspect a connection between her and this young man's unexplained arrival. If Papa had him in mind as a match for Mary, she'd have been far more vociferous about it.

William Dutton was comely, tall, fair locks waving softly almost to his shoulders, clean, regular features, skin so pale as to be waxen, eyes of the brightest blue, an expression as composed and near angelic as a man could be. Pretty as a maid, Frances concluded cruelly. But handsome? Handsome belonged to mature men, like Henry or Dick or John Lambert or – at the name her heart did a little leap of longing – Jerry.

'Young Master Dutton may have striking looks,' she said pertly, 'but I cannot say I like him.'

The disappointment on Mary's face only strengthened her suspicion that a conspiracy did exist, that her ever well-informed sister knew something more than she was saying.

'I do not like him in the least,' Frances repeated defiantly.

Sunday brought the consolation of Jerry's hand touching her and the sort of kisses that transmitted their need through every fibre of her body. No longer avoiding her, he was even more ardent, possibly because of the strain of separation. No doubt, she concluded but did not ask, he'd had some worry on his mind too private to tell her. Oddly though, the fact that they'd never again gone as far as they'd done in that empty room was a relief to her for all she longed for him, and maybe that had played on his mind too; maybe, like she, he feared the danger in it, the likelihood of being discovered should it have continued.

Now, as they parted after all too brief a time together, for her the next Sunday could not come soon enough. She wasn't to know that they would not be at Hampton Court that next Sunday, nor the next or even the next. Suddenly all visits ceased and it wasn't the weather preventing them, which in the autumn of 1653 was clement enough.

The road had admittedly grown difficult no matter which route would have been taken. Due to her father's concern of plots on his life, his method of travel was always varied. Travelling by horseback would have overcome the slithery mud but Mama only rode on firm ground, maintaining that she was no longer young and a tumble could be disastrous. They could have gone by river, the water smooth as glass under a calm autumn sky, but that too was ignored. Instead they spent their Sundays at Whitehall but a few steps away.

No reason was given, certainly not to her, and not even the all-knowing Mary knew except to say how boring it was just walking across the road to Whitehall Palace to hear their Sunday sermon.

Jerry was now at Whitehall, but it was as salt rubbed into

a wound that with the place so busy she could only see but not touch. He gave fewer sermons from the pulpit of the palace chapel, so even drinking in his lovely resonant voice was denied her much of the time.

Whitehall was no Hampton Court. With its staterooms and offices and the great Banqueting Hall designed by the late Inigo Jones, who'd died last year aged eighty, it was no weekend retreat. In the heart of London it was a thoroughfare for all sorts of people on all sorts of business. Seclusion had no place here, no secret nooks for lovers to meet.

Here the sense of being watched was stronger, though she told herself not to be silly and over-imaginative. Yet the question nagged – why had Papa terminated all visits to Hampton Court yet had allowed Jerry here? Was it to keep a better eye on them, catch them together? A silly thought – he with all his great affairs of state behaving like a skulking schoolmaster. And yet . . .

This thought was in her mind even as she made her furtive way to the one place they still felt safe – a small courtyard, one of many. Jerry having given her the most furtive of directives, there was no choice but to follow at a distance, her heart pounding like great hammer blows with anticipation, and experiencing a small moment of panic when not sure which direction he had taken until she glimpsed him again going out through a small door.

A cold November north-easterly wind buffeted her as she stepped out on to the narrow courtyard leading to the river. The place was deserted. One or two boats tossed on the grey, choppy Thames. Frances glanced up at the two blank walls at either side of the courtyard. The one behind her had only the door through which she'd come and two tiny windows high above her – as secret a place as could be found.

The wind eddied down into the area bringing with it the

sooty smell of chimney smoke. She shivered. There had been no time to throw on a cloak and hood. She almost leapt out of her skin when someone moved in front of her as from nowhere. He'd been standing behind the door she'd opened on to the courtyard. Now he caught her to him, pressing his chilled lips to hers.

Held tightly in Jerry's arms, she let her fright melt from her and clung to him, his cloak folded about her slowly excluding the cold, and warmth began to pass between their locked bodies.

With time now to think, the joy became marred by fear. 'This is too dangerous,' she whispered, thinking how easily someone could come through the door from which she had just emerged. 'Someone will come.'

'No one will.' He kissed her but she wasn't calmed.

'My father has set spies on me. He knows. I'm certain he knows. He's closed Hampton Court to our family because of me.'

Jerry ceased kissing and looked tenderly at her. 'It's the New Assembly – the new Parliament – that has closed it. They have plans to sell it to pay for the war with the Dutch. The country is in debt, my love. Closing Hampton Court has nothing to do with us.'

She stared in disbelief. 'But my father loves the place. He'd never allow its sale. He *is* Parliament.'

'Nevertheless it is to be sold. By auction. Last month it was offered to him in exchange for New Hall at Thaxted, the Duke of Buckingham's estate that your father bought, but he wouldn't agree to it. So now it's being sold to help pay some of the country's debts.'

Frances shook her head. She knew now, it had been Papa's doing – to get back at her and her lover. Why else give up his favourite retreat yet hold on to that ugly place at Thaxted where the family never went? He could have sold that instead and had the whole of that beautiful palace by the Thames to himself, but he had refused.

'I must go,' she whispered urgently, angry that they'd wasted so much time together talking. It seemed he felt the same way as she. He leaned forward and took a last lingering kiss.

'Next week,' he murmured forcefully. 'Here.'

'Yes.' She needed to be gone. Quickly she pulled away and went back inside. She did not see the face pressed to one of those tiny upper windows, its casement fractionally ajar the better to overhear.

Twelve

The Nominated Parliament – 'Barebones Parliament' as it was being called after one of its saintly members, Praisegod Barebones, a one-time Anabaptist preacher – soon proved as much a failure as the Rump, though not for the same reason. Godly men striving to be too godly, reforms hastily made without weighing the consequences soon fell apart. Alarmed by the radicals' high-flown intentions, the conservatives stated that it was not good for the country, especially one fighting a war.

Lambert and his moderates drafted a New Constitution resolving to return to Lord General Cromwell the powers he'd given to Parliament. When the radicals, like the Rump, stubbornly continued sitting, it was Lambert who called out the Army to remove them. This time Parliament dissolved itself. The mace formally handed to His Excellency Lord General Cromwell with great pomp, on the twelfth of December 1653 the Nominated Parliament ceased to be.

Four days later Lambert handed his New Constitution to His Highness, as Cromwell was to be styled. An Instrument of Government, its purpose was government by one person with periodic Parliaments – in other words, a king. Although badly in need of a leader, with Cromwell the only capable man for the role, the country was divided – but no more so than the family itself.

Bridget wrote from Ireland that those who thought to

rise higher than the Lord God intended them to gave little thought to how far could be their fall. Henry, worldly and safe in government, was behind his father. Richard, as always, went on enjoying life with no particular worry other than how he was going to pay for his latest outlay – a fine Arab stallion the colour of bronze and a bright little filly of the same colour for Dorothy.

Betty greeted the news with her usual selflessness, happy for her father. Her mother said little, though anyone could see how her face fell at the thought of being queen, her simple roots shaken loose from the comfort of their humble soil. Frances too kept her thoughts to herself, shying from the prospect of becoming a princess. Mary thought of nothing else.

'We need someone to rule the country properly. None wants a Stuart back and Papa has long been regarded as the country's leader.'

With sleet on an easterly wind bringing a December afternoon to an early close, the three women sat in the cosy warmth of Mama's little parlour: Elizabeth on a velvet-padded armchair, feet on a velvet footstool while she sewed a frayed hem; her two youngest daughters on footstools before the fire, each reading a book.

Glancing up from her sewing, Elizabeth stared into the fire, its flames casting harsh, moving shadows across her small, plump features while the candles on the stand beside her cast gentler ones.

'I know your father well enough to know he will refuse that offer.' But Frances noted the tension with which she gripped her needle. Mary noticed nothing.

'He cannot turn down such an honour,' she said hotly.

Her mother shook her head. 'Your father never sought that honour, as you call it. He will protest and have his way as he does in all things.'

Mary clicked her tongue impatiently. 'He mustn't protest. It's the highest pinnacle a man could hope to reach.'

'The highest pinnacle, Mary, is to love the Lord above all else.'

But Mary was already being carried away. 'A crown has been offered, Mama. Not once but many times. How can he refuse when the country needs him so?'

Frances let the slim volume of French verse Madame Duret had given her on her birthday earlier this month fall idle on her lap. 'Papa shouldn't let himself be tempted,' she said firmly.

'And why not?' Mary turned on her. 'It isn't a sinful temptation.'

'It is if he forgets he is but the Lord's servant in what he does.'

'He has never forgotten that in anything he does. No one seeks the Lord more fervently than he in all his duties. Everyone knows he considers himself God's humble instrument. Who, Miss Piety, is a better instrument of God than a king?'

Frances knew too well what lay behind this sudden loyalty to Papa – Mary was smitten with the desire to be a princess. 'Not every king has been so,' she reminded. 'And please, do not refer to me as Miss Piety!'

'You behave so.'

'I do not—'

'Enough, please!' protested their mother, putting her sewing to one side with some force. 'I'll not have this quarrelling, and certainly not have you use the Almighty's name to further your quarrel.' She stood up and glanced down at the ornate octagonal gold watch she wore on her bodice. 'I must see Mrs Pearson about supper and arrange with Maidstone to go over the household accounts tomorrow morning. Now pray, be friends. No more bickering.'

But bickering had always been short-lived between them and as the door closed, Mary giggled.

'It's Mama's favourite pastime, I do believe, checking accounts and visiting the kitchen. She concerns herself over the last penny and the last bit of bread and never stops repairing old gowns as if we were in poverty. To see her none would believe us to be wealthy beyond dreams. Her frugality is public knowledge.'

Frances joined in with the joke but sobered quickly, picking up her book. 'Sometimes I do wish Papa weren't so wealthy,' she sighed as she turned the page.

She heard Mary give an irritable huff. 'What's wrong with us being wealthy?'

Frances didn't look up. 'What we once had should have been enough, but you want more, and so does he. He looks now to being king and you to being a princess. I'd prefer us to remain as we were.' The words on the page misted. How could she explain to Mall how she felt – Jerry and all? 'I wish we could be as we once were!' she blurted and lowered her head even more as though reading.

'Oh, tush!' Mary got up to walk about, throwing her arms wide. 'Look at this house – is it not a beautiful house? Right by Whitehall Palace, given to Papa by Parliament. Look at the people we rub shoulders with. Why, even Heren Beverning, the Dutch emissary, bade me good afternoon last week. Were I a commoner he would have passed me by.'

'We are commoners, Mall. We aren't yet royalty and may never be.'

But Mary was warming to her subject. 'Papa is having talks with him regarding the Netherlands. He says it's time there was an end to this war. People are so wearied hearing those great guns firing at each other off our coast. To think, Frankie, it's in Papa's hands to *end a war*! That's how important he is. And the Polish Vice-Chancellor, Rad . . . Radseseski . . .'

'Radzeijewski,' corrected Frances.

'He came seeking assistance from Papa to supply horses and a ship to help overthrow the Catholic King of Poland. Queen Christina of Sweden has written to him that in her opinion he should become king.'

'Queen Christina of Sweden,' put in Frances, 'is widely known to be a frivolous woman.' But she went unheard.

'And the Venetian Ambassador has also voiced that he expects Papa to take the crown. Think of it, Frankie – Oliver the First. How great we shall be.'

Frances put down her book to study her sister closely. 'You are far too fond of greatness, Mall.'

'And you are too wearisome for words!' Mary snapped, her joy in the subject vanishing like a popped soap bubble. 'I'm going to see when supper will be ready.'

In a huff she took herself from the room, leaving Frances to stare morosely into the winter-bright fire, alone with her thoughts.

Breakfast in the panelled dining hall done, Frances made to leave as her father stood up, but he sat down again as the others left and lay a firm but loving hand on hers, at the same time giving her mother a significant nod to leave also.

The hand compelling Frances to sit back in her seat as an inquisitive Mary was ushered from the room by her mother, he said, smiling, 'I've a few minutes before I leave for the House. I thought to give them to my own little wench and hope she grants her father a moment of her time in return.'

The thick fingers gently patted her slim hand. 'A loving father and daughter, Frankie. Seldom do we sit together at ease after a meal these days. I am so called upon of late, and you, as with all young people, are ever busy at your own interests as well as your tutorage. I take it both you and Mary learn well from our capable Andrew Marvell?'

Frances nodded obligingly and he gave a sigh of satisfaction. 'He is as fine a teacher as he is a poet, and in truth a great and inspired poet. I avidly read his work and was especially pleased with his tutoring of young William Dutton during his stay here. Now he has taken young William with him to stay with our mutual friend John Oxenbridge at Eton, I miss the boy as much as Mr Marvell. I am told he did learn well but like my young daughters was ever eager to be about his own pleasures.'

Resigned to the usual convoluted path to his point she waited. Beyond the latticed windows London was preparing for another working day. The Cockpit faced directly on to a fine square where a small market was held once a week, and with the winter sun not yet above the rooftops the call of stallholders could already be heard. Muffled by the closed windows came the rattle of carts, snickering of horses, bleating of sheep to be sold. The babble of buyers and maidservants sent by their employers filtered into the now quiet dining hall, itself dim in the soft morning light of a winter day before the sun would strike in to add gold to the dark panelling.

In those parts of the city where houses were so clustered together that sunlight was blocked out for most of the day, narrow streets and crowded alleyways seldom seeing the sun, her family was fortunate to be in an open part of London where the wealthy congregated.

Her thoughts wandering, Papa's voice had receded, but she was shocked back to it by the single word 'husband'.

She looked at him, startled, and his hand covering hers tightened reassuringly. 'An excellent one, Frankie, a gentle and modest young man of a like conscience to yourself. I speak of innocence, uncorrupted by experiences of the flesh.'

He was regarding her with such intensity that it seemed his eyes were boring into her very soul. Did he see there what she thought safely hidden? She felt her cheeks grow warm from guilt and prayed it be mistaken for maidenly blushes at such frank reference to knowledge of the flesh.

Whether unwittingly or by design he followed along the latter line. 'I've embarrassed my little wench. I am too blunt a man and have been too long in men's company, I fear, and easily forget the delicacy of women. Let us overlook that I have been so and speak again of young William Dutton. I am anxious to know your thoughts on him.'

The name made her heart sink but she held her emotions in check. 'I've not particularly thought of him.'

Oliver's smile was indulgent. 'Was he not a constant companion of yourself and Mary throughout the summer? Did you not consider him kindly in manner and courtesy?'

How could she say she could not stand him? 'But I could not find myself becoming fond of him if it is in the respect that you mean, Papa.' She fell silent, her eyes averted from the penetrating gaze.

'I did hope,' he said, disappointment in his tone, 'you would find in him such quality that would promote in you a strong affection for him over time. Tell, me, Frances, do you feel no smallest spark that might cause you to dwell upon thoughts of marriage to him?'

She held her silence and after a while he gave her hand one final pat and released her, standing up slowly to tower over her. His expression, however, remained that of a loving and tolerant father, and he stretched his sturdy frame as a man might after a pleasant rest.

'Then we will not labour the matter any further just now. I dare to say a thought has been sown in your heart that had most likely not come to you before. So leave it to be mulled over. And now I must away.'

Frances found Mary in her room. Mary looked shocked when she told her. 'Surely he can do better than William Dutton!' she said.

Her reaction surprised Frances, having expected to have to plead for her support. 'But you were only recently trying to encourage me towards him, babbling how handsome he was.'

'So he is. He'll make a fine and virtuous husband. But that was then, before Papa had any thought of becoming king. You really cannot marry someone as ordinary as William Dutton for all his father was titled and wealthy. Nothing less than a duke for you now. You simply cannot marry William Dutton. I will intercede for you.'

'Oh, no, Mall! Papa will be sure to think it a conspiracy.'

'He'll think nothing of the kind. I will explain it to him. Once he sees that a king's daughter could not possibly marry just anyone, he'll seek a far better husband for you.'

Misguided though it was, Mary's natural bent to take charge where affairs of the heart were concerned would at least give her time to draw breath. The longer she had the better a way might be found to coax Papa into looking more kindly upon herself and Jerry White. Frances prayed she had a loving enough father, king or not, who would see how sick at heart he would make her in denying her the man she truly loved.

On Friday the sixteenth of December in the year 1653 at one o'clock the procession began its progress to the Court of Chancery. There Cromwell would receive the sword of state and the cap of maintenance, that ancient ritual symbolising the authority of kings.

It was a marvellous procession: narrow, winding streets ablaze with colour on a dry cloudy day; the cavalry riding proudly, harnesses jingling, breastplates, back-plates and gorgets bright as mirrors; uniforms of buff, green, red, blue; foot soldiers marching in step, muskets shouldered, pikes held firm; the London Aldermen, a splash of scarlet robes; flags and standards fluttering alongside naval ensigns and City of London banners.

The route was thronged with excited spectators enjoying a diversion from their everyday lives. Held back by soldiers keen-eyed for trouble, the squash of humanity beneath the projecting upper storeys of houses was as tightly packed as sheep in pens.

Amid the colour and noise the solid figure of Cromwell, with the brightly robed Lord Mayor of London beside him in his coach, sat with quiet dignity. Black-suited with a white collar, the only colour he had allowed himself was a gold band around his tall, black, wide-brimmed hat.

Cromwell had gotten his own way after all. Frances couldn't help thinking of it with pride as she sat in one of the following coaches bearing the great man's family. Occasionally she glanced at Mary and felt her deep disappointment. Papa would not be crowned king this day. Instead he'd be solemnly installed as Lord Protector of England, Scotland and Ireland.

Even so, she wasn't sure whether to rejoice in this moderate compensation or not. In the past the title of Lord Protector had been reserved for the guardian of an infant king too young to rule alone, or of one non compos mentis, ruling in his stead, perhaps only temporarily but a ruler for all that, whose word was law. This time it was surely more than that – there was no infant, no king too insane to rule, just Cromwell alone, king in all but name.

By the time the procession gained the Court of Chancery, however, Frances forgot to question as pride in seeing this enormous family of Papa's gathered together in one place took over from scepticism. But as the lengthy ceremony grew ever longer, Papa speaking the solemn oath to take upon himself the protection and government of the nation, Frances began to lose interest and gaze slyly about at those of his family gathered to honour this great occasion – all were here except his ailing mother and Bridget, who had refused to attend what she saw as defiance of God's scheme of things in regard to kings.

The Cockpit had bulged with them as they'd gathered in readiness for this day. His five sisters – he being the only brother – were all present. His recently widowed sister Catherine Whetstone, a gentle, dependent lady, had been offered permanent residence and was so grateful that she crept around the house keeping out of the way like a little mouse. There was his sister Elizabeth, who had never married and lived with another sister Anna and her family. There was Jane and her husband John Desborough, a large lumbering man of grim face and rustic manner, an Army man through and through; Robina the youngest, who with the death of her first husband, a canon of Christ Church, was now married to another divinity, Mr John Wilkins, with whom Papa was on the friendliest of terms for all his Anglican cloth.

Of the closer family, Betty looked drawn. Frances fell to thinking that the green velvet cloak and hood she wore made her look even paler; Dorothy too since the loss of her baby, Ann, last year. At least that rich burgundy silk took away some of her wan looks. Richard of course was like seeing royalty itself, so flamboyant he looked. Henry too had resorted to overdress, while his beautiful wife Elizabeth shone in mulberry satin, an outer wrap of dove grey with a sable fur collar and muff.

Beside all these fine clothes Frances felt drab. Mama had insisted her two youngest daughters remain quiet in their choice of dress. For herself she had chosen a most sombre slate-grey, plain-woven, silk taffeta with a wide, white cowl collar that made her look more like a maidservant than Her Highness the future Protectoress.

Mary voiced her disgust in a guarded whisper halfway through the proceedings. 'We look like three poor country folk. To think we might have been princesses but for Papa's high-principled notions of duty and humility. To tell the truth, at this moment I am feeling every bit of his humility!'

Even so, from the moment of their father's inauguration as Lord Protector, both she and Mary found themselves being addressed as the Princess Frances and, to Mary's delight and satisfaction, the Princess Mary.

He might well have been king, for within the month Hampton Court Palace was hastily repurchased for the sole use of His Highness. By April Whitehall Palace had become their London home. As they once said goodbye to the little house in King Street for the Cockpit with all its opulence, they now bade that place goodbye for Whitehall with all its pomp and grandeur.

Thirteen

1654

'Isn't this the most splendid room you've ever seen?'

Mary flung her arms out in a single sweep to embrace the bedchamber whose furnishings and furniture had once graced Stirling Castle: rose silk Damask drapes, the same fabric repeated on footstools and window seats; wallcovering of pink watered silk; carpets the finest Turkish; side tables, chests, bedposts all beautifully carved.

'I swear I shall never find sleep here for looking at it all the time. And look! A dressing room too.'

Frances watched her antics. Her own room was equally splendid in sky blue, her favourite colour, with silver and gold threaded through the materials. 'Mama has certainly displayed excellent taste,' she remarked.

But not all of her mother's ideas had been met with similar joy. For weeks Whitehall Palace had resounded to hammer and saw in the altering of the residential quarters. The great staterooms, audience chambers and the magnificent Banqueting Hall, with its painted ceiling glorifying the monarchy, had been left untouched, but she had disapproved of the vast rooms that were to be their personal quarters and ordered they be partitioned to form smaller, cosier ones.

'How can she spoil such a beautiful place?' complained Mary as they stood in what had been an expansive drawing room with painted ceiling and fine panelling while work men laboured around them, rich furnishings piled into corners. 'I'm sure she'd be far more at home in some cottar's hovel.'

To some extent Frances was on her mother's side, her own position promoting a kindred spirit in this need for simplicity.

'Vast draughty rooms might suit kings,' she said, 'but Mama is a practical person. Smaller rooms retain warmth in winter. She does so crave cosiness that brings a loving family closer.'

'But we're as near royal as any could be,' persisted Mary, hardly ever able to keep off the subject. 'Mama can be so embarrassing . . .' She broke off to dodge a passing labourer. 'She is being lampooned even in the London broadsheets.'

'They write anything that will draw readers,' said Frances. 'At the same time Mama is criticised as mean and over-thrifty, Papa is accused of spending great sums of the country's money upon he himself.'

But she knew the latter criticism was justified – thirty-five thousand pounds on furnishings alone. In a way it seemed symbolic of the wedge being driven between this family and the people; more alarming, between her and Jerry. All the wealth anyone could want would be hers, while he remained forever on a stipend unless Papa chose to lift him up, which would depend on how favourably he viewed his young chaplain.

Stuff was being brought in from Stirling Castle, Nonsuch and from storage in the Tower of London. A long procession of craftsmen, upholsterers and workers in silk and linen drapers, men to clean and rehang the great pictures retrieved from the late King's effects, Mantegna canvasses, Raphael cartoons – it was all too grand. Frances wondered anxiously at her father's changing taste to the ostentatious where once it had been so plain.

As the army of workmen and craftsmen left, in came coachmen, grooms, wardrobe keepers, a personal waterman for Papa and a host of servants high and low. The sister of his old valet, Jean Duret, became one of Mama's maids of honour, the nephews becoming pages.

Frances now had her own lady's maid, Margaret, a gentlewoman of pleasing countenance and dainty ways. Mary too had her personal maid, Ann, of similar disposition to Margaret. Poor Lettie, whose artless manner and untutored speech no longer suited, was relegated to less public parts of the palace though more than happy with her rise in wage. Mrs Pearson retired with a fine pension, her place taken by a master cook, Mr Philip Starker, renowned for his skill in preparing banquets. Mama missed not being allowed to cook any longer – in a way as relegated as Lettie – and Frances knew how sorely she missed her chats with Mrs Pearson, Mr Philip Starker abiding no one, not even Her Highness, interfering in his domain.

Much of the previous staff, old retainers, jobless and homeless and left to fend for themselves after the death of the King, had lurked in holes and corners over stables and workshops in Whitehall Mews ever since. Turned out of their palace quarters, they found themselves again evicted from their hovels; too old to work or unsuitable with their hordes of brats, they were paid off with next to nothing so that the Mews could house the Protector's coaches and Arab bloodstock purchased by him from abroad.

'How will those poor people live?' Frances asked her mother, her heart sad for them. 'It was the only home they knew. Could they not have been provided for as was Mrs Pearson?'

The reply was simple. 'Mrs Pearson was in our employ. These were in the old King's employ, to whom we owe nothing.'

'They cannot be blamed for his misdeeds, to be turned out so cruelly.'

'They should have departed when the King did. But they clung on like leeches, erecting miserable dwellings as to make the place unpleasant to the eyes and foul to the nose, living from hand to mouth by begging, not seeking employment to cause better conditions for their children.'

'The children,' reminded Frances. 'Can Papa be so unfeeling as to turn little children out to beg their bread?'

At this her mother's face grew sad. 'There will always be beggars, my dear. Can your father provide for every last beggar in the land?'

'Then need he add to their numbers?' Frances challenged heatedly. 'He has had reserved for him thirty-five thousand pounds from the King's belongings to be spent on this palace while those poor souls have nothing. Could not a little have been spared for them?'

'And what of the rest of the poor of this land – how far would it go were he to use it all on the poor? When it is exhausted the return to their old ways would be the worse for having partaken of better food for a few days, for that is how long it would last. Your father would need regular countless thousands of pounds to permanently improve the life of every poor man in this country.'

As Frances turned away, her mother caught her by the shoulder, making her turn back. 'But take thought to this, Frances – the money your father has been granted is not his to fritter as he pleases. It is state money to maintain a large royal residence, and what has been spent so far is a great deal less than would have been squandered by Charles Stuart.'

Chastened and in the face of such logic she had no argument, and though she felt for the poor people of the Mews it wasn't long before more opulent people found themselves turned out of the palace itself – members of the

Admiralty Commission obliged to vacate their apartments for her brother Dick – now referred to as Lord Richard – and his family when in London.

It was 1654 – half the year gone already and as far as Frances was concerned, proving the most wonderful of all.

The war with the Netherlands had been amicably settled and with more time to himself Papa was again spending weekends at Hampton Court, the close air of a London summer with its risk of smallpox and other noxious fevers making it essential. Thus she was with Jerry again, with plenty more secret places to meet than at crowded Whitehall.

She was sixteen, approaching marriageable age and meant to be innocent of lovemaking until taught by her husband, but she already knew that joy, though not a breath of it to anyone – even to Mary, with whom she had always shared every confidence. Frances was starkly aware that this time her sister would never be able to keep a thing like this to herself.

In the hidden places where she and Jerry met they'd talk of their hopes of her father eventually melting towards him. Jerry had told her about his meeting with her father and the outcome. She had upbraided him. 'How could you? It was a silly thing to do. Now he's been alerted he may have his spies watching us even now.' She'd looked fearfully at the door as they stood together in a darkened room, imagining someone outside listening, but she was too much a coward to have him open it lest her fear be proved.

He'd defended his action saying that they could not continue forever in this way, that he intended to marry her no matter what. They had gone on quarrelling in whispers, their first ever quarrel, until finally he'd taken her in his arms and calmed her with kisses and lovemaking. Later she'd regretted time wasted in fighting, for it was difficult enough to meet these days without that.

Hampton Court had become a crowded place; it was indeed becoming a royal court. The long summer brought hordes of guests eager to fawn about His Highness, among them the Lamberts and the attractive Countess Dysart, who was growing more scandalous as time went on, exactly as though she still existed at court.

For all she was the wife of Sir Lionel Tellemarche, the Countess of Dysart had clung to her own title inherited from her father William Murray, who had been the King's whipping boy in their youth and for his pains been given the title of Earl of Dysart.

At Hampton Court she loved playing the gallant with His Highness Cromwell and he with her, lapping up her overtures, jesting with her, dancing attendance with such affectation that watching it, as did most others, Frances endured waves of embarrassment for him.

'What a fool Papa makes of himself,' she hissed to Mary. It was made all the worse by the fact that he dared play the protective father where her own life was concerned and all the while showing himself up in public. 'Even Mama has noticed it. I've seen her press her lips together whenever she sees Bess Dysart. It must be so humiliating.'

Mary shrugged, too busy playing princess to care about Mama's feelings.

Betty, ever ready to see no ill in anyone, defended her father, saying he'd always been one to display his affections openly. Dorothy was no ally either, too wrapped up in her children – three-year-old Beth and eighteen-month-old Mary, a somewhat sickly child and still on a wet-nurse.

'I've no time to concern myself with your father's tomfoolery,' she said. 'It's quite harmless. Men do have their silly diversions. They are but boys.'

But with a sense of ever being watched by him, Frances could not feel so light-hearted about it. She sought Henry but he playfully pinched her cheek, saying that he had more to think about with Elizabeth expecting in September than to worry about his father's antics.

If Bridget had been here she'd have rallied to her side, and for the first time in years Frances wished Bridget were here. Though how she'd deal with her and Jerry – were she ever to find out – she dared not contemplate.

It was almost midsummer, the hottest day so far. Ladies wore their lightest dresses of voile and lawn and lace, cream and fawn the dominating colours. They congregated across the lawns of Hampton Court like posies of faded flowers, their short curls and tender faces shielded from the sun by wide-brimmed hats similar to the men's but of lighter materials as they gathered to watch the morning sport their host had laid on for them.

'What would Bridget say to all this?' Frances scorned. 'I hear she and Charles haunt Baptist meetings in Ireland.'

She watched the smooth flight of a falcon change to an accurate and deadly swoop, dropping like a stone on to a partridge, bearing it to the ground. The spectators applauding, the falconer hurried to lure the bird from its prey with a gobbet of raw meat, the falcon already depluming its kill with its hooked beak.

'Bridget would tend to dull the enjoyment,' was all Mary said as she applauded with the others.

Dorothy was fondling little Mary's fingers while the child snuggled against the breast of her wet-nurse taking little interest in her mother.

'I'm told Bridget is developing a taste for fashion and colour, so she cannot be so dull and prim as once she was.'

Losing interest in the conversation, Frances watched the man bring back the dead partridge to add to the growing pile and wondered where Jerry was. Sunday morning and she'd not even seen him at this morning's sermon, and her gaze encompassing the lawns could see everyone but him.

There was her aunt Catherine on the arm of Colonel John Jones. She had regained confidence and would soon be leaving widowhood behind. He cut a splendid figure in blue and gold Dutch breeches and jacket, as did most of the men, even Papa in a gold and plum-coloured suit. Richard was in white, gold and cherry red with bows and frills and fringes and with plumes on his hat. Henry, though, was dressed sombrely and appeared more the man than Richard ever would.

John Claypole was in a short sea-green jacket, shirt blousened out under a darker green fringe, Dutch trousers to match and a tall, narrow-brimmed hat of the same green as the tassels on his breeches and jacket. The Lamberts were in amber satin and brown velvet, she with a high-crowned hat like a man's topped with soft brown and gold feathers, and in a riding jacket and skirt. Countess Dysart too wore riding habit, bottle green – too warm a colour for such a hot day, Frances smirked. But the smirk faded as her gaze found the one for whom she was truly searching. A little removed from the main groups, he was talking with two other ministers.

As though by the draw of some magnet she saw his head turn, his glance move in her direction. Across the lawns their glances now met above the motley gathering and even at this distance each interpreted the other's message. In a while they would wander away from the present company and seek out the meeting place pre-arranged from last week – the fountain designed for her father by Fantelli, near to the statue of the naked Cleopatra.

He'd had the gardens restored, reaping complaint from local people in channelling the water from the artificial Longford Water constructed by King Charles which had flooded into surrounding farmland. During the civil war farmers had broken it to restore their fields but now it was open again to feed the two Hare Warren ponds in Bushey Park and the fountains of the garden.

It was behind the Fantelli fountain that Frances and Jerry had found a little arbour caused by the natural enclosing of shrubbery and it was there they would meet this afternoon. The warm sky would be their only witness. He would be gentle and unselfish, he knowing her most intimate parts, though he would do nothing that she did not wish and at all times cared for her well-being. It was always wondrous, and he had sworn to make her his wife come what may – only a matter of time and patience. In the deepest throes of their love she knew he'd never give up that quest, that between them they would finally overcome her father's prejudice.

London on the third of September 1654 was again treated to a fine spectacle – the opening of the first Protectorate Parliament, as near a royal occasion as any could possibly be. In the Painted Chamber of Westminster Hall an elaborate gilded chair, grandly spoken of as 'the throne', had been elevated upon a dais for His Highness with a table in front of it.

The route to Westminster, cordoned by blue cloth with streamers and flags flying and with drummers and heralds, was a sea of spectators. From the carriage carrying her and some of the family, Frances could see only a blur of faces, London pale, while the ride seemed to take an eternity. With her in the coach were Mary, Betty and John. The one in front bore her mother, Richard and Dorothy, and in front of that, a most gorgeous coach carried John Lambert, her brother Lord Henry and Papa resplendent in a suit of russet-brown velvet extravagantly embroidered with pure gold.

Thousands of Londoners had swarmed to see him pass, yet he hadn't pleased all. The day was one of great significance – the anniversary of his triumph at the battle of Worcester three years previous. That it would fall on a Sunday had made no difference to his plans; it was a propitious date and the procession had gone ahead despite public opinion. In deference to it, however, the proceedings of Parliament would be brief and most of its time spent listening to a sermon in Westminster Abbey, the main business left for Monday. But as far as Frances was concerned it was a waste of a precious weekend, and she was glad when it ended and they were back in Whitehall. Around the hearth they toasted bread on the trivet, buttered the hot slices to pass around, enjoying the informality. There was hot buttermilk to sip and spiced mulled ale for the men. The room was warm and conversation became sleepy.

Oliver had been quiet for some time, staring into the fire, and it was Betty who noticed and brought everyone's attention to the sleeping Protector, his pipe lying loose between his fingers, his head lolling, and he had begun to snore. Elizabeth leaned towards him and touched the hand drooping over the arm of the chair.

'Oliver, my dear.' As he awoke with a start and a querying grunt, she went on, 'His Highness needs to seek his bed.'

He blinked awake and with an effort collected his wits, heaving himself upright in his chair. 'Forgive a weary man for retiring early,' he said.

'Your father's years call for an easier life,' Elizabeth said sadly as he left. 'But the country has greater claim on him.'

Indeed all his time promised to be taken up wrangling with this new Parliament – papers to be read and signed, decisions to be made, ambassadors and other foreign visitors to be received. If Frances knew anything about her father he would work harder than any king ever had.

* * *

Henry's Elizabeth had been brought to bed, her first child soon to be born. Apprehension roamed their Whitehall apartments as in any house with a birth imminent. With a thin drizzle and low clouds making the September afternoon more like evening, supper some way off and Oliver not expected home for some time, the family was startled by his bursting in on them.

'Outside all!' he ordered, his face sanguine. 'Follow me!'

Before he could be told that the physician was already with the expecting mother, he was ushering everyone along the corridor and outside towards the Mews, servants hurrying after them with cloaks against the drizzle.

'There!' he stated as breathlessly his family caught up with him. One arm theatrically outstretched he indicated six of the most well-matched greys Frances had ever seen. 'Frieslands. A gift from the Count of Oldenburg.'

'They are beautiful,' Betty exclaimed in delight.

'I think so too.' He flung an arm about her. 'We'll all go to Hyde Park to put them through their paces.'

'We cannot,' cried Elizabeth. 'Henry's wife . . .'

'Ah, Henry!' he called as though seeing him there for the first time. 'I shall need you with me on this.'

Henry's avid gaze took in the spirited animals. 'I would long to go with you, but I must remain nearby my wife at this time.'

His father frowned, then his brow cleared. 'Has her time come?'

'It has,' broke in Elizabeth. 'Brought to bed this afternoon.'

Beaming, he slapped his son on the back. 'Well done, man. I look forward to the birth of my grandson. I've had enough of girls in my family, a host of sisters and a host of daughters, though each is dear to my heart. But I long for some new little man by me. Remain with your charming wife, Henry, and by the time I return I pray the Lord will have delivered her safely of a son. Now!' He turned briskly to the others. 'Who's to accompany me to see these fine beasts put through their paces?'

Elizabeth shook her head. 'I must stay here by my daughter-in-law.'

Betty too declined. 'I shouldn't be out in this weather, Papa. But John will go with you.'

'Most certainly,' agreed John.

'Good. Well said.'

'May we too?' Mary cried, including Frances in her request.

He gave a shout of laughter, as tuneless as his voice. 'Such a tomboy do we have. Then you shall. But not to ride with me, you understand. These are untried and also the coach needs to be light. I shall handle them myself but need another to assist me should they become too restive. Not you, John, for I would never face my sweet Betty again if hurt should come to you.'

Elizabeth gazed anxiously at him. 'If you are so uncertain of those beasts, Oliver, should you not let some other person handle them?'

Oliver's snort was derisive. 'I've handled horseflesh all my life and know what I am about. My trusted John Thurloe there will sit beside me.'

His eyes alighted on the slight figure of his personal secretary hovering a short way off. Small, fastidious, with a calm mien, prim-lipped beneath a fair, drooping moustache, he was his employer's eyes and ears, his shadow, his spy; in fact paid an army of spies to guard His Highness against harm. Oliver trusted him implicitly, turned to him with any problems he had. Of high intelligence, Thurloe was the son of a clergyman. Meticulous as to detail, he was intensely loyal to his master. Frances had never been quite at ease in his presence. She now felt somewhat dismayed at his coming with them but there was little she could do about it.

With the team harnessed to one of Papa's fine coaches, he sat at the reins with John Thurloe beside him while she, Mary and John Claypole in a similar coach followed behind to Hyde Park. There were only two hours of daylight left but the sky was clearing, though the drizzle had left the wide track bordering the open fields of the park very muddy. People had begun to venture out for a stroll, and seeing His Highness pass, lifted their hats or dropped a curtsy and politely applauded his handling of the splendid team.

People gathering watched the first run, his expert handling drawing more applause, as turning the team under such muddy conditions proved something of a feat.

'He's so skilled with them,' Mary was remarking when they saw the coach skid and lurch sideways a little.

The unexpected movement panicked the horses, who were already nervous in strange hands. Throwing up their heads they started forward, each fighting the other's gait. The reins jerked in Oliver's hands; horrified, the crowd saw His Highness dragged bodily down. Instinctively grabbing at him, Thurloe too was thrown off. At the same moment came a loud pistol shot.

The explosion of Thurloe's pistol as he hit the ground came at the same time as Frances screamed, seeing her father's hand fly to his head. The reins twisting about his foot, his body was dragged bouncing like a rag doll alongside the pounding hooves.

Suddenly Oliver's shoe came off, releasing him from the enmeshed reins. He lay immobile as Thurloe picked himself up and, together with alarmed onlookers, raced to where the Protector lay. Running with the others, Frances pushed through the throng, her heart pumping with fear as she gained her father's side. To her utter relief she found him sitting up.

'I thought you dead,' she sobbed, throwing herself at him, Mary all but falling on him as she too rushed to cuddle him.

'I heard a pistol fire. I thought you shot.'

He gave a shaky laugh as he held them both to him. 'Indeed, so did I. The ball went by my head. I felt the breeze of it.'

He winced as willing hands helped him to his feet. 'But I think I have done damage to my leg a little. Your father will walk lame awhile. A fine state of affairs for a country's ruler.' Jokingly he brushed aside Thurloe's profuse apologies as he allowed himself to be assisted to the other coach, the gift of horses and his own coach to be brought home slowly by his secretary and John Claypole. But joke as he might, by his own hand he had been made to look a fool before the people.

Soon those with Royalist sympathies were making much of it in not too particular broadsheets, calling him an ill-advised coachman who had undertaken to manage three kingdoms and that bad driving would lead to bad ends. His supporters, however, spoke of his miraculous escape as a sign of God's satisfaction in their leader; as the Venetian Ambassador put it, had he been killed the country would possibly have been stricken into another civil war.

Fourteen

Young Elizabeth's baby was born two days later – two days of struggle that made the family wonder if either would survive. Her cries echoing through the private apartments, Henry was distraught. 'Dear gracious God, she has done no harm in her life yet to be so torn in pain. It takes so long.'

'It is her first,' comforted his mother. 'It is always the hardest.'

'Could I but take away her pain, I'd feel less guilty.'

'She is in good hands, Henry. Your father's physicians are the finest and she is strong. With God's grace she will give you a strong son.'

Her conviction calmed him and several hours later he was gazing down through eyes full of grateful tears at a little daughter while his wife smiled wearily up at him from her sweat-dampened pillow.

'We shall call her Elizabeth,' he murmured lovingly, even though the family was already teeming with Elizabeths, 'after her brave mother.'

In November he, his wife and new daughter went to stay with her parents at Chippenham in Cambridgeshire.

'I miss them,' said Mary. 'It's become so dismal here.' But Frances chafed more at the dismal air of Whitehall in general.

Father had become unapproachable, spending long hours

at the bedside of his mother, whose frailty had worsened in the last month. It could have given Frances more opportunity to creep off to meet Jerry except that everywhere she went the dark watchful eyes of John Thurloe seemed to follow her. She'd often sense one of the many he paid to keep watch for her father's enemies following her. But Thurloe need not have gone to any such extremes – as her grandmother grew weaker, Papa fell into an ever deeper depression and had no interest in anything other than his mother, the whole family feeling the weight of his sorrow. As such it felt wrong to indulge in secret meetings with Jerry for the while and he agreed to it.

'We can endure the wait, my sweet Frances,' he said, though to her aching to be with him it sounded too lightly said.

'Your father has much to bear,' condoned her mother when Frances complained of his tetchiness, she too having come under its lash as he bemoaned the constant bickering of his Parliament while he was being so distracted with other things.

'There are times,' he had lamented to her, 'when I would rather keep sheep under a hedge than have to do with the government of men!'

Complaining of a painful leg from the coach accident as well as his need to be by his mother, he'd cancelled important engagements. He also put off a long promised visit to his dear friend, Richard Mayor – Dorothy's father – at a time when his presence might have been of comfort, for one of that family was also close to death.

Doctor Wallis faced the bleak eyes of Dorothy Cromwell, his own expression also bleak. 'I have to tell you, dear lady, it is a grave congestion of the lungs and the disease has taken great hold of her. I shall do what I can.'

'Do all you can!' Dorothy's distress was heart-rending

to see. 'She is but two years old. We cannot lose her. I could not bear it.'

She was nowhere eased by being told, albeit gently, that it was in the Lord's hands and all they could do was pray He look kindly on the child and give her physician the skill to save her. 'Why does He need my Mary when I need her more? He already has one of my daughters, hardly three months old. Can He not be satisfied?'

Richard's arm tightened about her quivering shoulders. 'My dear, blame not the Lord. The child was not strong.'

'Who else shall I blame?' she turned on him. 'We gave her all our love. She was no street urchin to die unloved in a gutter. Ann was well fed, well cared for, yet the Lord saw fit to deprive me of her. Now He casts His eye on Mary. What have I done that He should serve me so? Is He such a jealous God as to want all that I love?'

Dick's face twisted in disbelief at her wild words as Doctor Wallis moved towards her. 'Dear lady, God saw fit to take your daughter to a better place, where she is now rejoicing in the excellent health she never knew on earth.'

'He had no right! I loved her . . .'

With the rest of her words dissolving into weeping, she leaned against her husband, who nodded apology to the doctor for this outburst. 'She must lie down until she is herself again. Do what you can and I'll pray to God to see fit to spare her, but if you humanly can, save our sweet Mary. My wife has had all she can take of losses and miscarriages.'

Nodding sombrely, the man returned to the room, which emitted the heavy odour of confined heat and camphoric embrocations and steams used in combating pneumonia.

For days the child lay in a high fever, her skin hot to the touch, her breathing with that tiny catch at each painful breath. She'd had that dry cough for over a week and now

Dorothy tormented herself that she had not recognised it earlier as something dire.

'She has still to reach her crisis,' said Doctor Wallis, offering a crumb of comfort. 'We can now only wait – and pray.'

Hours later the parents and grandparents were summoned, creeping into the sickroom with its stagnant airs to sit by the bedside. Dorothy could hardly look on the pallid face so small on her large pillow, the body so tiny beneath the covers, the breathing so fast and shallow. She clung to the dry little hand, willing Mary to open her eyes and look at those gathered about her. Were she to, it would mean she would recover, Doll was sure of it.

With all her strength and her renewed belief in God's goodness she prayed for those round blue eyes to open and look at her – to dance again with life. But they remained closed. Softly closed, the gentle features seeming to her to already be taking on the subtle look of death, so subtly that it would go unrecognised by those who had never before witnessed death. But Doll had been given cause to witness it before and in sudden terror she looked up at the doctor, saw him shake his head, and even as she cried out, 'Oh, dear God, no!' she looked down to see one last tiny gasp before that little chest became still.

The hollow sound of Dorothy's weeping filled every corner of Hursley Lodge. There was nothing Richard could do for her, he himself too numbed.

Of the four children Doll had borne, they had but one living – Elizabeth, a strong-willed four-year-old who always managed to spurn Richard's every attempt at affection though she clung lovingly to her mother. But even her love did not now relieve Doll in any way.

The simple funeral over, the little body laid in the family grave in the tiny churchyard, the mourners sat on a while longer in prayer while above them the weeping continued. No one could offer comfort as Doll spurned all attempts, even her mother's.

'I know not what to do with her,' she said in frustration. 'We are all saddened. I loved her as much as did Doll, but it is ever so with children – we must expect to lose some of them.'

'She has grieved this way for every one of them,' replied Richard. 'As if God has struck at her alone and no other. She heeds not the Bible and its teachings of forbearance, patience and acceptance, but takes her loss as His cruelty towards her alone. I cannot reason with her.'

Richard Mayor noisily blew his nose. 'I've never understood this need for women towards copious weeping. It does no good.'

'There are many things you do not understand, dear,' Ann Mayor said sharply, turning the mourners' heads to her in amazement. Known for her fluffy and inoffensive nature, she wasn't one to rebuke anyone, much less her husband.

Family and close friends sat in awkward silence as her husband got ponderously to his feet and, giving her a small, curt bow, made a dignified exit. This wasn't the time to rise to any counter-censure.

It was little Mary's other grandfather, Oliver, who took it hard, it coming on top of his other woe as he shut himself away to be with his dying mother.

'When she has gone to the arms of Our Lord,' Elizabeth Cromwell said to Frances, 'which after eighty-nine years on this earth being ever pious and kindly is well earned, your father will no doubt be himself again.'

As November came to its close on a quiet, misty night, his mother died, conscious to the end, with her family about her. Turning her head feebly on the pillow she gazed at her only son as he knelt by her holding her frail hand, tears flowing down his florid cheeks. She tried to touch them with her free hand but had not the strength.

'The Lord cause His face to shine upon you,' they heard her faint whisper. 'Comfort you in all your adversities and enable you to do great things for the glory of your most high God and be a relief to His people.'

Overcome, he dropped his head upon her hand and a little later she spoke for the last time, her old voice again barely above a whisper. 'I leave my heart with thee, and goodnight,' and her eyes closed, content with their final sleep.

There was a day of national mourning. On a cold, damp, dismal Sunday evening the long funeral procession wound its way to Westminster lit only by hundreds of flickering, slow-burning torches to the muffled roll and tap of the drum while Cromwell as chief mourner walked slowly through the soft intermittent drizzle.

It was well after Christmas before Oliver was himself again. But the old humour had left him. The father that Frances had once known was gone.

All through the days of mourning she hadn't seen Jerry at all. But by February she was once again in his arms, though their secret courtyard was no longer the best or most comfortable of meeting places in this place of eyes.

In February her personal maid, Margaret, brought her a message saying that her father wished to see her in his study. Papa's study was well removed from the household apartments. It was where formal business was done and it brought concern to Frances.

'What can he want by such a dour message?' she asked Margaret.

A tall, friendly, well-bred girl of nineteen, Margaret had become her confidant. Frances had even trusted her enough to open her heart in regard to her and Jerry – an intrigue in which Margaret readily shared. She often kept watch so that their time together might not be so fraught in this very public Whitehall Palace. She'd even suggested he come to her mistress's bedchamber, though Frances shrank from that as being too bold and a little too dangerous. Snatched moments in some summer arbour or winter courtyard was one thing – in one's own boudoir was another entirely.

At the moment Margaret's face was one of concern. 'I haven't been told, but it could have to do with your nearing marriageable age. You are in your seventeenth year, Your Highness.'

'Please don't call me that,' begged Frances, having often in the past requested her not to.

'Be on guard,' cautioned Margaret, glossing over the small rebuke. 'Your father is not of a mood to tolerate imprudence even from you, my lady – it could cause him to make decisions you may regret.'

Frances returned the steady, meaningful gaze. 'I will be prudent.'

He was sitting taking his ease by the fire when she entered, the room a large, oak-panelled one with a desk, shelves, bookcases – the symbols of his work – but retaining some comfort with Turkey rugs, expensive paintings and rich if masculine drapes.

His smile was weary as he patted the low stool beside his chair for her to sit on. He looked lonely – the highest man in the land, its ruler, its virtual king, sitting alone in a chair by the fire. Her heart went out to him and she ran and dropped a loving kiss on his forehead, noticing as she did so that the hair had thinned, making that forehead higher than it had once been.

The ruddy complexion was showing lines of care. The nose – the butt of the country's more ruthless wits – looked even more robust than usual. The heavy, striking features had become merely heavy, and that once hardly noticeable wart above his right eyebrow had become far more prominent. Her father was growing old. Yet his voice, for all its weary tone, was strong and commanding even in affection.

'I am ever amazed to see the pretty young woman that my little wench has become,' he said as she sat by him on the stool. 'I fear your womanhood has come too swift upon me. As I grow older the years pass ever faster – as if the grave can hardly wait to be filled.'

Her resolve was momentarily forgotten. 'Oh, Papa! Don't speak so!'

There was a sudden glimmer of amusement, the father she'd once known shining through briefly before he became serious again. He gazed about his office.

'I apologise for the formal aspect this place appears to present. It is the only place where we may not be disturbed – always some member of the family about our own private apartments, ever needing my attention over some trivial matter. See, I have some wine for us – a fine sherry sack.'

He indicated the delftware jug on a side table, two small goblets and a silver dish of sweet biscuits. 'And those jumbals to nibble with it. We need not be over-serious.'

Frances curbed the impulse to query the reason for this summons and the silence drew itself out; father and daughter sitting together before the fire, needing no conversation, as if in mutual ease. But she knew it wasn't that kind of silence and it was he who broke it first, his tone musing.

'It comes with a sense of anxiety, fear even, that a man suddenly finds his daughter nearing the time to leave him for another. In part also, a foolish jealousy for that fortunate man, whoever he be.' He gave a small chuckle. 'This sounds like I am reproaching God in His great scheme of things, but we are mere mortals and cannot help our feelings, and though we suppress them knowing ourselves wrong, they are always there with us – in fathers.'

Could he be referring to Jeremiah White? Did he know about their meetings? Was he condoning them, at last seeing where her heart lay? Certainly his tone wasn't one of reproof. She dared to hope. But she needed to proceed with caution. 'I have thought many times of how it would be to be wed,' she stated, staring fixedly into the fire. 'Though I have not yet spoken of any man whom I wish to marry.'

'Ah, but in a year perhaps. Eighteen is a sublime age for a maid to wed, and you will be that before you can blink an eye, does time go so swift. And now comes the time for my youngest daughters to think of future husbands while they are still in the bloom of youth, for too soon that first bloom fades, never to return.'

His fingers were fondling her curls in an abstract manner. Her father went on, 'A woman is like a rose – first the unopened green bud sheathed in innocence, then comes the first peep of colour, blushing and timid, enticing the hand to touch its delicacy. Then slowly it unfolds to he who chooses it for himself. After that it will open fully, sweet to the senses, and for a long while remain so, accepting, ripening, swelling.'

Yes, she knew only too well that this was how it had been between her and Jerry. But did her father also know?

'But finally,' he went on, his tone grown sombre, 'as with all of us, the colour fades, the petals fall. In some they may remain awhile, loose yet clinging to the stem, but at last they too will fall. They fall . . .'

The voice wavered, became silent. Frances forgot Jerry and looked up at him questioningly. Tears had welled up in the heavy-lidded, grey eyes. Now they slipped quietly down his cheeks, and she suspected he was thinking of his mother. In an effort to comfort him she covered his large hand with her slender one. At the touch he drew his free hand across his face in a rough gesture of embarrassment to sweep away the moisture that had betrayed him.

Sitting straighter he cleared his throat, withdrawing his hand from hers. 'Memory is not always a man's comforting companion. But I digress.' He was again himself. 'The truth is that I have asked to see you to help me with a problem I have. A short while ago I was entrusted with the will of an old colleague of mine, and now comes the time when I must abide by the wish contained therein. Yet something in me says to stay my hand until I seek advice on the yea or nay of its contents. I need your help with it, Frankie.'

'I will help if I can.' Frances felt a mixture of disappointment that it had veered from marriage – possibly in connection with Jerry, whom she was sure he knew more about than she had given him credit for – and relief that it had not been a censure of her after all. It was like him to begin by worrying the life from her only to end upon something quite innocuous.

'First I must read it to you,' he was saying, 'so you may understand my dilemma.'

He got up and took down a rolled parchment from a nearby shelf. Returning to sit down he unrolled it and began to read aloud.

> 'I humbly request and desire that His Highness the Lord Protector be pleased to take upon himself the guardianship and disposal of my nephew William Dutton and of that estate I by Deed of Settlement have left him, and that His Highness will be pleased, in order to my former desires and according to the discourse that hath passed betwixt us thereupon, that when he shall come to ripeness of age, a marriage may be had and solemnised betwixt my said nephew, William Dutton, and the Lady Frances,

> His Highness's youngest daughter, which I much desire and (if it take effect) shall account it as a blessing from God.'

He looked up. 'You see my quandary. I hesitate to urge you to consider the young man, but a will is a thing to be honoured, as any dying wish.'

Stunned by what had been read out, her heart froze within her while her soul shrieked out against the shock of it. She managed to find her voice, hearing it raised in anguish and fury.

'It was *your* promise, Papa – it is not mine! You can't honour such a promise on another's behalf even though she be your daughter. I will not take the young man!'

He was frowning as though perplexed. 'What's amiss with him? He is of pleasing countenance and impeccable manners. He has no blemish or deformity. He is not debauched. True, he may not be a wit as some are. Nor is he rakish, or lusting after higher things by consorting with one such as you—' – he broke off, seeming to change his mind – 'as *some* may, Frances.'

The words were so pointed. She stared at him, surer than ever that he knew more than he was saying, this last connotation and the way he had used her full name even more proof. He knew about her and his young chaplain. Yet his expression remained as bland as ever and she could only go on with her own charade.

'There is nothing in William Dutton,' she said as evenly as she could, 'to cause me to find no fondness for him, but I cannot find love for him.' In sudden desperation she clutched her father's arm, caution leaving her. 'Please, Papa, do not condemn your loving daughter to a life of misery with a man she could never love.'

He was silent for a moment while she gazed imploringly

up into his face. When he spoke his voice was low and deliberate.

'What do you know of love between man and woman, you being young and innocent? Remembering, Frances, that God sees all.'

It couldn't have been more direct. It could only be that he saw the knowledge she already carried concerning love – its ecstasies, its agonies, its power to raise a woman to the heights of heaven then dash her into the very abyss of hell, and all the while not for one moment allowing her to wish her life again without that one who stirred her to such love.

She said no more and he let her go, but she knew now that the radiance of that love she bore for Jerry White had shone for a moment in her face, revealing her secret more surely than could any spy in her father's employ.

Fifteen

1655

In her bedchamber Frances turned to her maid. 'What am I to do, Margaret? Everything I do is known. I have not dared to go near Mr White since.'

Margaret had stood listening in silence to her mistress's tale, but now it was time to speak. 'You could be mistaken. After all, my lady, you did not confess it in words that day. It could be you are imagining things.'

'I am not imagining things! My father hasn't taken this country by the neck, seeing into the heart of every man, only to be ignorant of his own daughter's movements. I was a fool to think otherwise. But I cannot give up my beloved. If my father comes between us and sends him away I think I shall die. But how can I get word to him now and not put our love in peril?'

Margaret regarded her thoughtfully as Frances threw herself down on her bed in a fit of misery. 'If I should take a note for you . . .' she suggested, but her mistress's voice came back angrily, muffled by the coverlet.

'How can you be so stupid? Everyone knows you are my personal maid. I might as well go myself for what good you can do.'

'Even so, he should be alerted, a message got to him. Who else is there you can trust but me? Not Lady Mary, who cannot keep a silent tongue in her head. There is no one but me. If you truly love him then it is a chance you must take. I will be discretion itself.'

Sitting up slowly, Frances dried her eyes with the back of her hand. 'You are a good friend, Margaret. What would I have done without your help these past weeks? Yes, you must take a message to him. But what do I say? I cannot think beyond telling him I love him, that my heart aches to see him, that I cannot—'

'Yes, Your Highness,' interrupted Margaret, in charge of the moment. 'But it must be a message of some direct benefit to you both, arranging a meeting place where you can safely speak together at some length of your plans. I would say here in your chamber, where there will be no interruption and I will personally keep watch for any—'

'Not here!' Frances regarded her in alarm. 'Never here. How often must I say it? It would be quite improper – and dangerous. For both of us.'

'It is the safest place. Who would ever think you so improper as to entertain a lover in your own bedchamber?'

'Margaret, I am not—'

'That you are not, my lady.' Margaret smiled understandingly. 'But the purpose will not be for love's luxury but to discuss earnestly what you both must do. Here is the only place for it. None would dream to look here.'

Frances had to admit, it was the most sensible solution. She let her shoulders slump. 'Very well. I expect you are right. Bring him here then.'

It was as though a great block of stone had been lifted from her. The risk was terrifying, of course, yet now that the decision was made, she felt better for it. Her father had left them time to decide what to do; they could make plans to creep off together and be wed somewhere secretly. And there was not a lot her father could do once they were bound together in solemn matrimony. Even Papa would never go against God's holy laws. He may be head of this country but he was not God's anointed king to feel himself right in undoing what had been done in the sight of God. At last, here was the solution to all those furtive meetings.

The curtains were half drawn, not only against the fitful sunshine of this March afternoon, but against prying eyes in any opposite windows.

Frances sat in an elbow chair near her bed and waited. Her fingers tightly clasped, her heart felt as though a flock of starlings were beating their wings inside it.

She had chosen a simple green dress, the bodice cut low, and a minimum of decoration – no rings, no necklace, just a pretty brooch to heighten the colour of her eyes. As Margaret had said, this meeting wasn't for indulging in love but for earnest discussion. Yet her heart still pounded enough to choke her, knowing that her bed was so near. It could so easily call to them, and at this moment she felt that should he express a desire for her in that bed she would be willing for it to be so.

The waiting was becoming endless. Then at last the door opened and there he stood. Frances brought her clasped hands up to her bosom, her whole body tensing. Even in his minister's black with its wide white collar, he looked like a young god, lithe and lean and smoothly handsome – like one of those depicted in the great tapestry covering the wall of her bedchamber at Hampton Court – and her heart leapt with love at the sight of him.

Margaret had planned it well. She would remain outside, ready to warn should any approach or a nearby door open. Before any could come near, she would enter as though having herself just arrived at her mistress's door. But she did not anticipate any trouble, the family being scattered about the palace on various pursuits: Mary taking the balmy spring air in the gardens; Mama at her usual pastime, either supervising something or entertaining her many visitors looking to get to His Highness through her; Betty, who was staying here for a while, was visiting friends; and, it being Monday, Papa was busy with some meeting, later dining privately with the attendees.

With no reason for anyone to be in this vicinity at this time of the day, not even servants, all appeared well.

For a moment Jerry stood by the closed door gazing at Frances, his sensual scrutiny sending small tingles of pleasure through her. When she held out her arms to him he needed no further encouragement.

Covering the width of the room in six or seven swift strides, he knelt before her as though to receive a blessing, kissing her hands again and again, and when she knelt down beside him he lifted his head to cover her throat with the same ardent kisses. Hardly able to breathe for the joy they gave her, she lifted her head the better to offer her breasts to his lips.

But they were here to discuss a more serious subject, which it took all her willpower to remind him of, and he moved back from her a little so that only their hands entwined.

'Of course,' he whispered, his dark eyes surveying those breasts as if longing to uncover them. 'There'll be time enough, my sweetest heart, for making love when we are away from here.'

To which she whispered hungrily, 'Oh yes, my darling, oh yes,' and brought his entwined fingers back to her breasts for one more moment before the cold business of discussing their elopement began.

While Jerry crept into the room of Cromwell's daughter, His Highness was sitting at table in another part of Whitehall Palace, surrounded by his Army officers. Every Monday he gave a dinner for them as had become his custom. This was the one day of the week when he could truly throw off the cloak of responsibility, the burden of disillusion that ever seemed to weigh heavier on him with each passing year.

He had been forced to dissolve yet another incompetent Parliament incapable of coping with the problems of state. This time their downfall had been caused by the Cavaliers and their cursed Sealed Knot Society seeking to restore Charles Stuart, and also the constant harassment from the troublesome Levellers.

In a rage, Oliver had told its Members that they'd allowed weeds, briars and thorns to flourish until finally he'd had enough of their tomfoolery and had dismissed the whole bunch of them. And now, once again the full burden of a nation rested on him alone. But better by far than that useless flock of honking geese he'd called a Parliament. Better by far to have military men about him who knew how to deal with a given situation. He recalled his Model Army during the civil war. He had made those men. They had stood beside him, straight and true, never faltering. He could rely on every one of them and could do so again.

Mellowed from a full meal and many glasses of ruby claret, his gaze moved languidly from one face to another. All good officers. All good men. These would take the place of Parliament. They might not be the most diplomatic, but while they looked after the state he could deal with foreign policy well enough. Ah, how he enjoyed these Monday dinners.

He saw Colonel Okey, a large, red-faced fellow, raise his goblet in his direction. He smiled and raised his own, tossing back its contents while all around him the Banqueting Hall rang with conversation and laughter – great guffaws of laughter.

It was said by those with axes to grind that his officers' dinners were mere excuses for drunken orgies; that he caroused and played the fool, unbecoming to a head of state. But kings had done worse. He did not for one moment excuse himself. In truth things did turn into noisy revelry on nearly all occasions, with more food being thrown about than was eaten, wine being tossed over the heads of fellow officers, men filling their friends' boots with wine and pudding or dropping a hot coal down another's breeches until the whole room was turned into a beargarden. But what harm in it? No worse than in Queen Elizabeth's time.

Oliver filled his goblet – so much so that the wine flowed across the table – and took a deep draught. Those who called him drunkard and unfit to govern, let them look to their own shortcomings. He had given his blood and his tears, his very soul to this country – so let this one day of the week be his.

'I can do more for this ungrateful country drunk than any dozen of them can do sober!' he roared to the man beside him, who had been taking the wine jug for himself. 'Damnation to our enemies! Damnation, I say!'

Rising to his feet as much as he was able, he lifted his goblet high. All around him the toast was heartily echoed.

'I've brought this country of ours to the very forefront of Europe,' he shouted above the cheers. 'Princes come now to seek audience with me. Kings bring me gifts – cloth of gold, tapestries from Italy, marble statues from Tuscany, glass from Venice, horses from Aleppo, even a leopard from the Sultan of Morocco.'

He sat down heavily to think about it all, gazing into the blood-red wine. He'd never set foot outside this country apart from Ireland, yet his name was spoken from Russia to the West Indies. His advice had been sought concerning the war between the Turks and the Republic of Venice. Envoys from Sweden, France, Poland, Norway, Italy, treated him like a king.

He seldom received people at Hampton Court other than one or two favoured guests – Bonde, the Swedish Ambassador, for instance, and Nieutpoort of the Netherlands, invited to share a friendly weekend. But at Whitehall foreign visitors were required to bow at the door of the Presence Chamber and again halfway into the room and finally on the lower step of the throne, while he, the nation's ruler, acknowledged each bow with a formal inclination of the head. What utter tomfoolery! What had happened to humility? What profit was it to rule a world yet lose his soul?

'Who would play the king?' he yelled, but no one took the slightest bit of notice, all too drunk.

He took a pear from a nearby fruit bowl, spilling its contents, and hurled it across the hall at John Lambert. It smashed into an ornate pillar, flesh and juice spraying all within range. This was a signal for a bout of fruit-throwing – apples, pears, peaches, plums, most of it imported out of season at great expense for his table. At the height of the fun, a footman came to whisper in the ear of His Highness. Instantly Oliver's face flushed, grew straight and stern while the merriment went on unabated.

'Where?' he blurted the single word.

The footman bowed and indicated the far door where stood John Thurloe and a thin, plainly dressed man.

'I'll come at once,' said Oliver tersely, suddenly sober. Leaving the revelry, he hurried to where Thurloe stood with his spy.

There was little need to probe into the why and wherefore and how long the informer had been employed at this present task. He already knew.

All he said was. 'You shall be amply rewarded for your work, as truly as the man in question will be most amply punished.'

*   *   *

It was impossible to discuss anything rationally with Jerry so close. She now sat on the chair by the bed, he kneeling before her, and with his lips so close to her bosom she could think of nothing beyond wanting to cling to him, to have him lean forward to kiss what flesh peeped coyly above her bodice. But plans had to be made and this time it was he who kept his head.

'On Thursday I am to return to Hampton Court to prepare a sermon for the weekend. I have no idea why your father wishes me to give it rather than one of his more senior chaplains, but there it is. But it does give me time to sneak away and return to meet you here in London. No one will miss me. This cannot be done here or at any weekend when your father is present. It is almost as though he wishes us to elope, it is so simple.'

He would have gone on instructing her what her role would be, but he was holding both her hands as he knelt before her, his lips close to hers, and she couldn't bear it. Gently she bent and brought his fingers up to her mouth, needing to wear down his resolve as she took them sensuously into her mouth, her action rousing her needs all the more.

They had not the wit to spring apart as the door flew open. There in the doorway stood Margaret, her face tense. Behind her like a great bear stood the Lord Protector, his gaze fixed on his kneeling chaplain. His voice came low and menacingly calm.

'What is the meaning of this posture before my daughter?'

All Frances could do was stare transfixed at her father, but Jerry had collected his senses immediately. Slowly, almost leisurely, he stood up and terrified as she was, Frances felt a rush of admiration for his coolness.

Apparently unflustered and self-possessed, he stood at ease before her father's damning enquiry. When he spoke his voice was even, while she was left still sitting where she had been first discovered but now trembling from head to foot, unable to say a word.

She saw Jerry switch his glance to her maid and honour her with a small bow before looking back at his employer.

'May it please Your Highness I have for a long time courted this young gentlewoman. She is my lady's woman and therefore I was humbly beseeching her ladyship to intercede for me.'

It came to Frances how clever and quick-witted he was in the face of this frightening situation, while all she could do was to sit petrified. Even as she expected her father to yell 'Liar!' a surge of pride went through her that her lover could maintain such presence of mind in the face of overwhelming authority. Jerry would master this business and bring them through it.

His Highness had moved slowly into the room, guiding the girl before him, but his manner now was kindly as he addressed her.

'What is the meaning of this, lady? This young chaplain is my friend, you know, and I expect you should treat him as such.'

Confused by being so spoken to, the girl's cheeks flushed and she dropped a low curtsy, her eyes demurely downcast and her reply flustered even though Frances could see that the girl's sharp wits had already understood the situation and she would go along with the subterfuge.

'If Mr White intends . . . intends me that honour,' she stammered, 'I . . . I should not oppose him.'

Subterfuge or not, Frances heard her own sharp intake of breath at her maid's forwardness, but if the gasp had been heard by her father he gave no indication. It brought a feeling of unease and she rose to her feet in the realisation that something was beginning to go vaguely awry.

Gazing from one to another she was aware of many things at once: the immutable face of her father's little secretary, Thurloe, behind him in the dim passage, his face looking like a disembodied head because of his black clothing; Jerry's innocent expression; Margaret biting nervously at her lip; but mostly the deceptively amicable demeanour of her father as he began to take over the situation.

'Well, young woman,' he said amiably to Margaret, 'if Mr White intends you such honour and you do not oppose him, we will have my secretary go and call Goodwin. This business shall be done presently before I go out of this room.'

Not once had he looked at Frances, and in the silence that fell over them all they waited while Thurloe hurried off to find the minister. In the meantime His Highness wandered casually over to gaze out of the window, first smiling cordially at Jerry, then giving his daughter's cheek a fond pat while Margaret stood back to let him pass, her eyes downcast, neither she nor Frances daring to allow their eyes to meet.

Not knowing what to do, Frances sat back down in her chair. The cheek her father had touched so gently felt cold and she could still feel his hand as surely as if he had slapped her.

She wanted to cry out that this was all nonsense, that it was she whom Jerry was claiming for his wife, that she was prepared to sacrifice everything to be with him – her home, her family, even her father's affection for her. She tried to catch Jerry's eye so that he might be the quicker prompted to speak up gallantly for them both, which she knew he would do before it became too late, but his face remained averted from her.

His face looked very pale. His expression was still impassive, those normally smiling lips compressed into a thin line. He was no doubt hiding the turmoil that churned within him. But she knew his thoughts without his having to look at her.

When the minister did appear, Jerry would step across and take her hand and declare that this was the woman he truly intended to wed in this very room. What could her father say but yes? Taken off balance and loathing to be humiliated before his secretary and minister, he could only give his consent. It was a clever move on Jerry's part and again her heart swelled with pride of him. In a few minutes all would be well. Here in this room she and Jerry would be married, her father's heart melting towards them both in seeing the strength of their love.

She had expected the waiting to be drawn out and was amazed when within minutes Thurloe was back with Doctor Thomas Goodwin. She half rose from her chair but then sank back as her father took Margaret by the hand to lead her into the centre of the room. It was not yet time. She must wait for Jerry to give her the signal.

Bidding John Thurloe to come in as witness, His Highness instructed the door to be closed then nodded for Jerry to come forward.

Now is the moment, Frances thought feverishly as the man who had her heart came to stand beside the young woman. Now he will leap away from her and present me instead. But as the seconds drew themselves out, he remained where he was while her father and his secretary withdrew to one side and Doctor Goodwin came to stand before the couple to begin the short and simple civil formalities that would join the two people together.

Helpless and confused, she could only watch, hoping that at the last crucial moment her lover would cry out against it. He must, he will, cried her heart as she sat tensely waiting for that moment to come. The room seemed to be spinning about her, making her feel she might faint, and she gripped her chair arms so as not to. All her faith was now pinned on Jerry's perfect timing – pinned on that moment that never came.

She saw the minister step back, his task done, the register signed. She saw her father take a small, bulging, cloth purse that Thurloe had handed to him and present it to the bride.

'This is for you, my dear, the lady's dowry,' he stated convivially. 'Five hundred pounds to see you both well settled in your life together, and may the Lord's blessing be upon you both and upon the very many children you will have. Amen'

With that he slapped Jeremiah White heartily on the back. 'And now my good friend, now that you have had your desire granted, I trust you will remain in my service for many years and I can look forward to your continued and loving friendship and advice as my chaplain.'

Jerry's reply fell like a hammer blow upon Frances, who was still clutching the arms of her chair.

'That I will do, sir.'

In all this he hadn't once looked towards her, but as her father turned to his secretary, ready to depart, Jerry's eyes met hers and a light of helplessness stole into his and the shoulders gave the faintest of shrugs as though to say, *What could I do?*

As for herself, her entire body felt numb, her mind no more alert than a clod of earth. She was vaguely aware that the room had become empty and very, very quiet except that the tapestried walls were absorbing the muffled sound of sobbing – a woman sobbing for the man who should have been her gallant knight, defying all comers to gain her hand, but who had proved to be nothing more than a cowardly betrayer.

Summer always brought its usual burden of fevers to the narrow, airless streets of London to claim victims, but it was still too early in the year for this. So it was with some perplexity that Doctor Goddard viewed his languishing patient.

Frances hadn't risen from her bed for over two weeks even though in that first week she'd been threatened with dire results if she didn't make some attempt to stir herself. When these threats made no impact on her, her mother grew worried, then alarmed, and insisted her father's own physician be called.

'I confess I am mystified,' admitted the man to the anxious mother. 'She runs a slight fever, but her complaint of nausea appears unfounded. Nor has she vomited at all during this malady. I can find nothing essentially wrong but for this persistent lifting of the temperature and her constant complaining of headaches. I am sure it is nothing serious and she will be herself very soon now.'

The slight rise in temperature and the headaches were of course caused by constant and secret weeping, and when the condition continued to linger, Mama's concern faded. 'It's time you made some attempt to combat this strange ailment,' she admonished in the end.

Frances clung moodily to her silence and only when Mary added her disapproval did she retaliate, her tone far too robust for one so unwell.

'Do you accuse me of pretence?' she snapped.

'I know you've been ill,' returned Mary, 'but more from lack of spirits, as far as I can see. You've had Papa greatly worried by it.'

Lying in her bed, Frances gave a bitter grimace. 'What does Papa care for me?'

'More than you imagine, Frankie. You don't see it, lying here pining and moping, your face all swollen with weeping. Little wonder you complain of headaches.'

Mary knew all about the business that had taken place

that day, and so did Mama, though she had chosen to say nothing of it.

'The man's not worth it,' continued Mary. 'Better you thank Papa for showing you his true worth now. He is not deserving of your tears. What if you had married him only to find out his little worth too late? Papa opened your eyes to the coward that he was.'

'But I know he loved me,' wailed Frances.

'No doubt he did. Men seem able to fall in and out of love more easily than we. Doctor Jeremiah White obviously had all the requisites that please the fair sex and without doubt knew how to use them to his best advantage. How dared he to think to become son-in-law to the Lord Protector? He was using you, Frankie, and you were too blind to see it. When he fell foul of Papa and took fright, he merely took an easy way out.'

'He loved me, but he was powerless to do much else.'

In reply, Mary took her hand. 'Try not to demean yourself further. Come, sit up and show that you are strong – that you are a proud Cromwell and will not be put down by such mean trickery. I will pray for you, Frankie, that you will try to show him that you care not a fig for him. Now, do sit up.'

Too despondent to argue, Frances slowly complied but kept her eyes lowered. But she was beginning to see the wisdom in Mary's words. To go on this way would be to lower her sense of self-esteem even further than it already was – to the satisfaction of Jeremiah White, if he thought about her at all.

Suddenly, she lifted her head, a new determination flooding over her. She *was* a Cromwell, as Mary had reminded, and no Cromwell had or would ever allow himself – or herself – to be put down by any man.

She would follow that practice and get on with her life, and, no matter how much it hurt, to hell with Jeremiah White!

In time she would put thoughts of him aside. She'd never forget him, but would be stern with herself whenever the mind wandered in that direction. In time she would marry, and marry well, bear children to the growing strength of the Cromwell family.

With these thoughts, lips compressed with renewed determination, Frances turned a calm and resolute face to the future.